One Simple Question

M. Shea Lamanna

LIVE LIKE CODI

One Simple Question

M. Shea Lamanna

To order additional copies of this book, contact:
Xlibris Corporation
1-888-795-4274
www.Xlibris.com
Orders@Xlibris.com
89978

University of Maryland Junior Writing Competition

Applicants must be ages 14-17 at date of entry. Writing Samples must be submitted no later than April 10th, 2006. Applicants must write about a question that fascinates them or sparks their interest. It may be a question involving philosophical ideas, scientific questions, literary questions, or a question about a topic that they do not have any previous knowledge of. Applicants must answer their own question and mention the people and places that influenced their journey in finding their answer. They must also give recognition to the time frame in which they found their answer. Applicant's writing samples will be judged based on writing style, originality in topic, proper grammar, and clarity. First place winner will receive $5,000.00 dollars in scholarships. Good Luck.

Acknowledgements

Thanks goes to everyone who's inspired me including my father and mother, family, friends, my grandfather, Mark Whitney, Cecilia James, and Bob Parmentier.

Thank you Christina He for using your talent to take my story and put it into a beautiful image.

Chapter 1

It's just one simple question. The quiz said to underline the prepositional phrase. Genesis sat with her hands holding up her head. She stared down at her English quiz. She had been paying attention in class but this was one of the more difficult assessments. She looked up and stared at the other people in the room. Everyone's pen glided across the page as if this was as simple as spelling "cat" and "dog." She bit her lip and stared at the white sheet of paper. At the top of the sheet was her name, Genie Anderson. She went by Genie instead of Genesis. It was pronounced like Jenny not Jeanie. Across the room, someone cleared their throat. She looked up but the person was unrecognizable and each person seemed a million miles away. Her head was spinning. She sighed and stared at question number four. Her blonde hair was pulled back and she twiddled with a loose strand. Her green eyes sparkled as they scanned the paper. Her pale hand held her pen. The boy who sat next to her had a watch and it told her that 13 minutes had passed since Mr. Abrams had originally passed the test out. Thirteen minutes later and she was only on number four. She exhaled sharply and clicked the back of her cold metal pen, making the tip retract.

Why did this have to happen today? She already had the worst day so far this year. Her Algebra 2 class had received their tests back earlier this morning. On Genie's test was a big, red, seventy-four percent. A seventy-four percent was a low 'D' at her school. It wasn't the actual grade that bothered her as much as her ex-crush, Mason, turning around and asking what her grade was. He, of course, was beaming and his brown eyes sparkled with the news of his ninety-six. When Genie had stared down at her test and looked back up at him, embarrassment and shame filled her. She opened her mouth to say something just as she did, the teacher spoke, "Everyone sit down, you know better than to share grades in front of me. Wait until after class please." Mason then turned around and flashed that perfect smile that had gotten her to fall for him the first time. Part of her jumped with his attention and the other part of her remembered the time she had wasted on him. The latter part made her angry and hurt. She had waited for him after class last year, when she had admired him. She had wasted her time, talking about him and helping him. All that he did for her, though, was make her jealous. He would act friendly but then walk away from a conversation to go and talk to another girl. However, right now she had an English quiz in front of her that wasn't going to complete itself.

She let out one last heavy sigh and then began to write. Underline this. Circle that. Label this, and done. When she stared down at the paper, all she could see was that she knew she had failed and it wasn't going to go over well with her mother. Sure, she was sixteen but that didn't stop her mom from treating her like she was six. She stood, pushing her hard wooden chair away from the matching desk. In her right hand was her quiz and in her left was a pen. As she made her way to the front of the classroom, the other students' eyes followed her. Her light blue and white plaid skirt swung with every step she took. When she had reached the front of the room she laid her paper on top of a pile that had everyone else's assessment. She pivoted away from the teacher's desk that was a messy array of papers. When she turned, she caught the eye of her best friend, Addison Moore. Addie raised a waxed brow in question. When Genie shook her head 'no', Addie nodded and mouthed silently, "same here." With that, Genie knew that she was not the only one who hadn't done so great on the quiz.

Addie had dark brown hair that had natural auburn highlights. Addie was a little on the short side standing 5'3 in heels. She was average weight for her age, which was about three inches taller than she was. This with her height, made her look naturally curvy. She had the thick hair that every woman dreamed of having. It was the same type of hair that you see in shampoo commercials that the models flip and shake around. That was the hair she had. Genie had always secretly wanted that hair. Of course, Addie had a natural skin color that made her look sun kissed all year round. Nevertheless, the most stunning part of Addie was her eyes. She had light, crystal clear, blue eyes. They looked kind of weird and misplaced on Addie but when she explained that her great grandmother had the same mysterious eyes that she did, Genie no longer thought they looked freaky but instead unique or flattering. Addie was the best friend anyone could have and Genie had never met any one quite like her. She was wild, loud, and totally unpredictable. Genie stared down at her navy blue sweater vest and pulled it down to adjust the bump that always seemed to form right where her vest and skirt met. It made every single girl look fatter than they were. She walked back to her desk and sat. Genie took her seat next to Michael. He had light blonde hair, just as she did. He had blue eyes and looked like every other teenage boy out there. He was just average. He looked up and smiled. He'd always been so nice to her. In his hands was a book that she'd read before and immediately recognized. She extended her French manicured finger out to the page.

"Have you gotten to the part where she leaves for home?"

She whispered so that only he could hear her.

"Yeah," he replied.

"I thought it was a shame that she didn't even say good-bye. I mean, after all that had happened and all."

Genie nodded, feeling her hair becoming loose from its clip. She reached back and touched the clip gently. He stared at her waiting to see if she'd add anything to the conversation.

"If you'd excuse me. We are experiencing technical difficulties," she said pointing to her hair.

She sauntered to the front of the room where her teacher Mr. Abrams sat reading a classic novel.

"Can I please go to the bathroom?"

She asked softly, not wanting to disturb anyone who was still working on that devilish quiz. Mr. Abrams looked at her from the top of his glasses.

"I don't know. Can you?"

This was the response she hated. Every teacher who used it thought they were the cleverest individuals on the planet. She knew that in Mr. Abrams head, he was praising himself for the snappy comeback to the very simple question. A little man on his shoulder was saying, "Go ahead, Mr. Abrams! You are one funny man. You should try for stand up comedy, you knee-slapping fool." She sighed and turned her head to the side.

"May I please go to the bathroom?"

He chuckled and responded, "Take a pass. Try being back before the bell rings as well."

She nodded and made her way to the hook where the passes hung.

In her school, they didn't have paper slips that allowed them to roam the halls. No, they had these little wooden paint stirrers that had either the words "bathroom" or "front office" painted on their sides. Genie had always thought the passes were a little ridiculous because in the history of the Blakeridge Academy, only one student had ever successfully cut class. Said student is referred to as a king. What made the private school so unique and difficult to escape from is that it had a mile long driveway leading up to the actual building. If you did decide that today you were going to rebel and cut class, you'd have to dodge teachers and curious students and sneak out one of the side entrances to the building. Once outside, you must walk to the front side of the school, all the while having to avoid windows where someone might, and most likely will, rat you out when they see you. If you manage to get 100 feet away from the main entrance without being seen, you must then walk (but if you are cutting it is a much better idea to run) or drive a mile to the nearest road where approximately 40 cars pass during school hours. So if the thought had ever crossed your mind to skip, you quickly remembered otherwise. The idea of having little wood pieces to prevent the students from skipping was a little far fetched. Either way, Genie made her way down the hall, skirt swaying with every step. Her tan Sperry docksides tapped rhythmically in tune with her swinging arms.

She thought about her job working for the town's newspaper. The Deal Island Gazette was the small town's newspaper that shared local news and displayed the elementary school student's art every other Sunday. It was a bit small and casual as far as jobs go but Genie was an aspiring journalist and whenever she applied for colleges, they wouldn't know what a small job it was, it just looked good on an application. Every week she had to go somewhere around town to write a review or brief summary about a local event. Every Monday and Wednesday, she stopped by the newspaper's little headquarters that just happened to sit on top of Genie's favorite coffee shop. It may seem like a silly hobby but it meant the world to her and writing kept her in control and she loved that. As she passed a wooden door and looked through the glass she was surprised to see a pair of dark brown eyes meet hers. The sight snapped her back into reality; she was still in school. Tyler Moore opened the door and followed right behind Genie. Tyler had those brown eyes that were so dark they almost matched his black pupils. He had long eyelashes and his dark brown, almost black; hair was cut and styled so that it looked windblown to the side. He was about 6 foot 3 and he towered over Genie. He had that almost permanent beach tan and Genie knew he had a six pack under his button up uniform shirt. In many cases, it seemed like he was the perfect 16-year-old guy. They were in the hallway, surrounded by white brick walls and navy blue lockers.

"So what are you doin? Skipping class?"

Genie smirked at Tyler's whimsical comment. She looked back at him and smiled.

"Actually," she responded, "I happen to be having a hair crisis, thank you very much."

He looked over to her and grinned, "May I assist you with your issue that way you can return to class as soon as possible. I'd hate to hear that you missed something important and know inside that I could have helped prevented that."

She closed her eyes as he stopped walking and gently pulled the clip from her hair. He handed her the clear plastic clip and smiled.

When they had been friends in middle school, he was awkward but still charming. Everyone was awkward in middle school though. I'm pretty sure Tyra Banks had a zit or two during her days of arts and crafts. Tyler had come out looking like a young man. But to Genie, there had never been anything there and there never would be.

"We missed you on Saturday."

She looked back at him to see him looking away. She thought about what he had just said. She had missed going to the movies with her friends and she did kind of regret it. Tyler was always great about coming up with catchy comments so she thought she'd try it herself, "Did we miss me? Or did you miss me?"

"Hey, whoa. Let's not get hasty here. I have a girlfriend. You and I both know that."

Genie smiled and stared down at her feet while they kept walking. She knew but she didn't like his girlfriend.

"You and I both know, also, that you can do a lot better than Lindsey."

Lindsey was your 'oh-so-typical' high school ditz. The long fake blonde hair with dark brown roots, hazel eyes, and the body of a cheerleader which is exactly what she was, a ditzy cheerleader. Genie had never favored her only because she knew that Lindsey was not particularly dedicated to her and Tyler's relationship.

"Well, excuse me. I am terribly sorry that I am not dating someone that you approve of. Fine. You and I . . . Friday night . . . my place . . . some eighties movies and all the popcorn your heart desires."

Genie looked up and her eyes met his and she didn't have to think twice before she answered.

"I'll bring the Dr. pepper."

Chapter 2

"Genie Anderson, I am so surprised to see you here."

Genie rolled her eyes and looked down at Alicia Rodriguez. Alicia stared back up at her with questioning hazel eyes.

"I would never expect to see you signing up to volunteer. Hell, this must be the beginning of the apocalypse."

Alicia grinned at her own obnoxious comment. Genie sighed and grabbed the pen that lay on the table waiting for losers who didn't have anything to do on the . . . 18th, to sign up. She glanced down at the first blank box and signed her name. Alicia sat in her cheerleading uniform and stared at her as though the words "Please, persuade me to do more, my dear Alicia," were written on Genie's forehead. Alicia just sat watching and smiling.

"What is this actually for? I mean, what will we be doing?"

Genie asked, stepping back from the table.

"What do you mean 'we'? Ha, I have better things to do on my Saturday than go to some homeless shelter. I hang out in Boutiques not mosquito infested restaurants. But don't get me wrong, I am so happy to see you signed up. It'll be a really wonderful experience." Alicia said the words, 'really wonderful experience' as though she were selling beauty products a group of housewives. Plus, homeless shelters weren't mosquito infested. Alicia was so ignorant sometimes, it was a wonder she passed the first grade.

Genie put on her best fake smile and walked away. Alicia had always been the girl that made all the adults think she was an angel that fell from the sky when really it was all an act. She was the president of five different committees. The only reason Alicia was president was so that she could go to meetings when she felt like it and no one was in a place of power to tell her to behave any differently. Committees looked great on college applications. Being the president of a committee looked even better. Genie wasn't the volunteering type, and she could completely understand why Alicia was so surprised. Genie hadn't volunteered at all. She didn't help out willingly nor did she join many clubs or decorate for the dances. She didn't like organized groups like clubs. They made her nervous and she thought they were kind of stupid too.

The reason she signed up for the Saturday the eighteenth was because that was the day that her older sister, Trinity, was coming home from college for the week. Her sister was the volunteering type. Trinity was a younger sister's worst nightmare. She was drop dead gorgeous, she spoke with proper grammar, played a lot of sports, acted and sang in the church choir, kept her bedroom tidy, never stayed out past curfew, and was never rude to mom. That was Trinity while she lived at home. Now that she was away at college it was a little easier but not much. Now, Genie heard all about how wonderful the University of Maryland was and how Trinity is 'just flourishing on her own.' Genie wasn't a bad daughter nor did she misbehave often but whenever your mom refers to your older sister as a goddess, it's a little tough to live up to that. Which is exactly why Genie didn't want to be sitting around the house whenever Trinity was telling tales of her castle at college park or a prince that swooned her in sociology. The mere thought of her mother and grandfather sitting around with stupid grins on their faces listening to Trinity tell about her freshman year in college made Genie want to runaway with the circus despite her intense fear of clowns.

The one thing that was keeping her sane was the thought of spending some time with Tyler before having to face her family's issues. Tyler was a great listener and would tell her things like, "Don't worry about Trinity, think, eventually you'll be in the spotlight and she will have no news." The thought of the comfort she would receive tomorrow night made her grin. Tyler was frequently at her house anyway. He had always wanted a little brother and Genie had always wanted to get rid of hers. He had kind of taken Genie's little brother, Noah, in as a friend. Noah was in the fifth grade and every time he saw Tyler's red truck pull up, he'd run out and hug Tyler's waist because he wasn't quite tall enough to reach his arms. Tyler and Noah's relationship was kind of sweet and Genie could always count on him being there if Noah needed a male figure in his life.

Genie's father had died four years ago. He had been diagnosed with Cancer when Genie was in the fourth grade. Victor had been a doctor and having someone else operate on him for a change, was difficult for him. For once, he was out of control and on the other side of the operating table. After countless surgeries, numerous doctors, and two years in the hospital, Victor Anderson's organs gave up on him. His lungs couldn't make it with tumors. Genie's mom, Ellen, had taken everything hard. She spent years mourning and it took a long time before she was able to come back to society. He had left enough money for her to send the children through private school and for the family to keep the house. When Ellen came back to society and got a job, she was singing of God's love. Genie's family had always been religious but whenever Victor had died, her mother couldn't go to church enough. Genie remembered Ellen saying something like, "There has to be a greater power up there if anyone expects me to move on. I'm gonna need strength and the only force in the universe that is great enough and can give me the support I need is God."

There were pictures of her father all over the house. Victor had blonde hair and hard blue eyes. He had an elfish face and there was something about him that made you trust and love him. Genie looked just like him. Trinity looked just like Ellen. Trinity had dark blonde, almost brown hair and light bluish green eyes. She was on the shorter side just as Ellen was. She had a heart shaped face and her hair had a natural curl to it. Noah was a mixture of Ellen and Victor. He had light blonde hair, light blue eyes, and freckles that were splattered across his face. When Genie looked in the mirror and saw her own blonde hair and dark blue eyes, she saw her dad in a part of her. She'd always been close with her father. She missed him.

Someone bumping into Genie in the hallway brought her back to reality. She turned to see who it was, Lindsey Davis stared back at her. She flipped her long blonde hair behind her shoulder and grinned. Lindsey's fake nails were so long, when they brushed along her cheek, Genie was sure they were going to slice her face. Lindsey stood before her in all her stereotypical glory. She had a fake tan that made her look more orange than tanned. She looked more than orange. In fact, she looked like and oompa-loompa who rolled around in cheese puffs. She had hazel eyes that showed not a shred of innocence. Instead they screamed 'liar' or 'slut'. It was hard to see if they said anything because she had a thick coat of mascara, eye shadow, and eyeliner surrounding those eyes. Lindsey was 5'6 and probably weighed about 100 pounds She was a stick figure and it was obvious that that's what she worked towards.

"I'm sorry, I didn't see you there."

Genie looked away as Lindsey spoke.

She quickly responded, "Same, it must have been your bleached teeth that blinded me."

Lindsey squinted and dodged a rushing freshman then returned her glare to Genie.

"You are just so jealous that Tyler picked me and not you. Have you ever thought maybe, just maybe, he likes to be around hot people? No wonder he avoids you. If I had to stare at that ugly muffin top of yours, I'd run too."

Could Lindsey get any shallower? Genie sucked in her stomach. Wait a second, she didn't have a muffin top and if she did, who cares? Lindsey didn't even give Genie a chance to respond before she pivoted on her heels and began to walk away. Lindsey's uniform skirt was so short; you could almost see her hot pink underwear when she walked. Genie groaned and turned in the opposite direction. Thank the Good Lord that it was the end of the day and she was getting a ride home from Addie. Addie would go off on a rant whenever Genie explained the confrontation to her. Genie walked a little farther before turning a corner and stopping in front of her locker. She quickly opened her locker and swung the door open. Inside was a folded piece of notebook paper. On the side that was facing Genie was written, "Genesis Hope Anderson" Genie could feel herself starting to blush and she quickly looked around her before unfolding the paper. Genie read the note to herself:

Genie,

Meet me after school tomorrow at the front of the building. I'll be standing by the fountain waiting for you. I'll give you a ride back to my place where we shall enjoy a night of Molly Ringwald and John Cusak. (Cusak's more for you;) But you have to do me a favor first. Try your best to be nice to Lindsey. She really wants to be friends with you. Oh, I almost forgot, don't bring any Dr. Pepper. Bring some chocolate sprinkles from your place; we're all out at my house.

Thanks.

Your love,
Camo.

Genie laughed out loud. The reason she called him Camo, was because when they first became friends in the sixth grade, all Tyler ever wore was camouflage pants and this awful camouflage baseball hat that he used to wear hunting. He looked just about as redneck as it came. She was sure that Jeff Foxworthy might make up a joke about his choice of fashion. Tyler had a nickname for Genie too. In his eyes, she was Glitters. She had been assigned the nickname because she used to be obsessed with sparkly clothing and glitter pencils. Deep inside, she still was.

They had become friends at the town's public middle school and whenever they found out that they would be attending the same private high school, their bond only became stronger. Tyler and Addie were Genie's best friends and coincidentally they were twins. The three of them spent hours together on the weekends. Tyler and Addie weren't always getting along but ever since Genie befriended both of them, they weren't just siblings, they were best friends.

Genie grabbed a few books out of the locker and stuffed them into her dark blue bag. Her bag had several buttons pinned to the cloth around the handle. A few different colored polka dotted ribbons were tied to the handle. Genie lifted the back and slung it over her shoulder. When she looked up, Addie was rushing down the hallway. She had a smile that stretched from ear to ear and several students watched as she ran down the hall. Her brown shoes made a thump on the wood floor as she ran. Addie wasn't large by any means but when you ran on the wood floor, you were bound to sound like a herd of elephants. She stopped right in front of Genie.

"You are not going to believe this."

Addie spoke with excitement bursting from each word.

"What's that,?"

Genie said shutting her locker door and turning to where Addie stood.

"Aidan Campbell . . . tomorrow night . . . dinner and a movie. I am hot stuff."

Genie laughed as Addie began walking toward one of the side entrances. Genie quickly followed.

"Aidan Campbell. Well then. What class do you guys have together again?"

"A.P. Biology. He's picking me up tomorrow at six. You should come over so you can help me pick out what I'm going to wear."

Genie looked down at her shoes than looked back up.

"I'll be there anyway. Tyler invited me over for movie night. Apparently you guys are out of sprinkles too," Genie said as she held up the crinkled note Tyler had left her.

"Oh okay. You have to help me first though. Tyler can wait . . . Wait a second. Have you and Ty ever been alone? Oh my gosh are you guys . . . wait what does Lindsey think of all this?"

Genie laughed and looked back up at Addison. Addie was pushing the door to the school open when Genie looked back to her.

"I don't know and I really don't care. She basically called me ugly today and said Tyler never wanted to be around me but she's just insecure."

Addie's jaw dropped. "Yeah well. Look whose spending Friday night with him, it's not the wicked bitch of the west."

Genie laughed and as the doors closed behind the two girls, she looked around the school grounds. Lindsey was standing with a group of guys, all wearing basketball jerseys. Lindsey looked back and glared at her. She thought about what Tyler had said about being 'friends' with Lindsey. Genie knew that she had all the 'friends' she needed.

Chapter 3

Genie stood outside the school staring at her knees as they shivered. She leaned up against the large stone fountain and waited for Tyler to emerge from the front doors. It was absolutely freezing outside and Genie considered going back into the building and maybe waiting inside the library where the large stone fireplace would keep her a little warmer than the hard, cold, stone that she was now clinging to. It was early March and usually it was beginning to heat up by now. There were about a hundred students on the front lawn of the Blakeridge Academy. Many were conversing with friends about the plans they had this evening and some were walking away to go to their cars in the student parking lot on the right side of the building. Then there Genie was, standing by the fountain that hadn't spurted a drop of water since late November. Addie was going to get some coffee and stop by her favorite boutique to pick up some new earrings after her last class. Genie bent over and reached inside her bag and retrieved a small plastic container of sprinkles. She stared at the little brown specks and smiled. Chocolate sundaes were always a tradition that accompanied movie night. Movie nights were the highlight of the week if no one had plans. Movie nights were make shift plans. They were assumed to be on if no one spoke of a date, party, or family event. As Genie stared at the ground, black converse entered into her vision. She looked up at Tyler. He had his black backpack slung over his left shoulder and his black sneakers were bar laced as they always were. She looked down at the sprinkles that she held and chuckled. He reached down and grabbed them from her hand.

"Ah, I see you got my note."

She smiled and stood, "How could I miss it. I saw the words Genesis Hope on a piece of paper and cringed."

They both laughed and began walking towards the student parking lot.

No one ever brought up Genie's full name. Genesis just didn't fit her and she wasn't particularly fond of it either. When she saw anything that said Genesis on it, she had to stop and take notice because it meant it was important.

"Yeah, I knew that would get your attention. So I picked up Pretty in Pink, Say Anything, and my personal favorite, Weird Science."

Genie groaned.

"Weird Science, hmm, if I wanted to see a bunch of horny guys, I'd take a peek in during Boys Freshman Gym."

Tyler laughed out loud and put his arm around Genie. She looked up at him and smiled.

"What makes you think only the freshmen are horny," Tyler said with a smirk on his face.

"Ew gross! Hands off!"

Genie said ducking so that his hand would fall from her shoulder. She took a few steps from him but then quickly rejoined him and they walked side-by-side laughing all the way to his car. Tyler pressed the electronic key making the lights on his pickup blink twice.

"Go ahead and get in. It's unlocked. I gotta go check in with Jess for one quick sec."

Genie walked around the back of the truck and watched as Tyler opened the driver seat door and threw his backpack into the backseat of the car. Genie grasped the chrome door handle and jerked the door open. She threw her bag onto the passenger seat and lifted her foot to the step. She grabbed the seat and pulled herself up. It was a very high truck and it was difficult to pull yourself up into it. When she finally got inside, she slammed the door closed in the attempt to keep the cold air out. She leaned back in the seat and sighed. She glanced over the truck and smiled. This was one of her favorite cars in the world. Tyler's truck was red on the outside and the seats and everything on the inside was black. There were a few pieces of trash lying around but for the most part it was clean. It smelled like Axe and Mountain Dew. Genie loved that smell even though it may seem kind of weird. She looked in the rearview mirror and watched as Tyler slapped some guy's shoulder and turned around toward the truck. Genie looked away as he started jogging towards her. Tyler grabbed the door and pulled it open. All at once, the cold air rushed in and Genie flinched. Tyler slammed the door shut and reached into his pocket for his keys. He jammed them into the ignition and started the car. He reached over and put his arm behind the passenger seat as he turned and backed out of the parking space. Once they were on the main road, Genie relaxed and leaned back in her seat. Tyler looked over and smiled.

"So how are your classes going?"

"Good. Nothing really new, I guess."

The school talk was always a conversation killer and never went anywhere. Genie sighed and looked back at Tyler. Immediately, she knew exactly what to talk about.

"Did you hear about Addie's date tonight?"

Tyler chuckled at Genie's question.

Addie was one thing they could always talk about with ease, "Yeah, Aidan something that starts with a 'c'. Ca . . . Car . . . Can . . ."

"Stop. It's Campbell."

Tyler made the puppy dogface, "But I was so close."

They both laughed and Genie continued, "Yeah, she is super excited. I'm gonna help her get ready before he comes."

"Yeah, sure. I have to give Lindsey a call anyway."

Genie rolled her eyes and looked at her hands.

"Speaking of which, where is your little love bug?"

Genie said love bug as if she was auctioning off an old car. She was close to singing that song that went like, 'Tyler and Lindsey sitting in a tree . . . K-I-S-S.' but she decided otherwise. He sighed and looked over at her with one hand on the wheel.

"She has to cheer at the basketball game tonight and believe it or not I really don't want to watch a bunch of dudes with their pants around their ankles run around for two hours."

"Genie responded, "Um, I believe that's called Basketball. Plus, Lindsey runs around in a skirt so short I'm pretty sure you can see up her ass."

Tyler laughed a hard and loud laugh that shook Genie to her core.

"A, I'm not gonna watch a bunch of jocks show off for each other for two hours so I can see her cheer or whatever for two minutes and B, I get dibs on seeing her in a short skirt anyway."

He smiled a fake little smile and watched as Genie pretended to gag.

The silence grew and Genie was happy to see the Moore house approaching. Genie had always loved Tyler and Addie's house. It was big and beautiful. It was a dark reddish brick with dark blue shutters. There were windows everywhere and beautiful stone steps that led to the front door. She never understood why the front door was so grandly decorated when everyone who knew the Moore's always used the side door. It had a detached garage and apartment up above the garage. Tyler got dibs on the room above the garage and it was a nice place. He had decorated it to be the ideal bachelor pad. It was every teenage boy's dream. Addie wasn't upset or jealous at all. She had said that she "had the rest of the place to herself." She had even made the comparison, "Huge house or tiny apartment on top of cold garage. I win."

Tyler pulled into the driveway and parked in front of the garage. Genie hopped out of the car not even grabbing her bag. Addie's cute little compact car was parked right next to where Tyler had parked. Genie ran to the side door of the house. She called behind her, "Be back soon Camo, have the popcorn ready!"

Tyler laughed and called after her, "Hey! You can't tell me what to do. Well I guess you can, but you know it's only cause I love you!"

"Yeah, yeah, yeah. Popcorn and sundaes!"

Genie screamed to him as her shoes hit the hard cold grass.

She burst through the door on the side of the large brick house. The door led into the Moore kitchen. Inside, Mrs. Moore was stirring something but Genie flew out of the kitchen so fast that she didn't see exactly what it was. Mrs. Moore had black hair and brown eyes. The black hair wasn't natural. She had died it what seemed like hundreds of times and it never did look right. She was on the petite side and her cheeks were so tight from smiling and treatments, that her face looked plastic She was a lovely woman and she loved her kids more than anything. Genie came to the large staircase that wound throughout the core of the house. She flew up the stairs two at a time. Genie held the end of the banister as she turned down to the right so that she could get to Addie's room. Addie's light pink door was at the end of the right wing. Genie ran at full force. Just as she was about to run into the pink door, Addie opened it. Genie rushed in and plopped down on the black and white, zebra striped comforter. She grabbed a pink pillow that was leaning against the headboard and hugged it.

"Okay, outfit?"

Addie did a 360 spin, displaying an artfully crafted arrangement.

"I. LOVE. IT"

Addie giggled and galloped to the three-way mirror she had in the corner of her room.

"You think Aidan will like it?"

Genie gasped and replied, "If he doesn't, well, you just won't go out with him again, simple as that."

Addie laughed and stared at her reflection in the mirror. She wore a navy blue dress that sat on her tan body perfectly. It was short but not too short and it covered everything that it needed too but it showed some cleavage. A thin, silver belt pulled in the silver flats that she was wearing and her silver studs were perfectly fitting. Genie watched as Addie sighed.

"You look great. And you are going to tell me all about it whenever you get back. I'll be here."

Addie smiled, her crystal blue eyes shining. Genie looked out the window and saw Tyler standing inside his room pacing, holding a phone to his ear. He looked worried or frustrated. It was hard to tell. Either way, Lindsey didn't deserve him.

"Okay, so the movie should be loading and . . . the sundaes are ready."

Tyler was messing around in the mini kitchen when Genie turned around to listen to what he was saying. Genie was sitting on the black futon that faced the large flat screen TV. Since first arriving at the Moore house, she had changed into jeans and a hoodie, helped Addie before her date, and rushed over to Tyler's just as Aidan was pulling into the driveway. Now, Genie was waiting as Tyler prepared the sundaes. She watched as he juggled numerous containers of toppings and tried to get the popcorn out of the beeping microwave. He had a steaming bag of popcorn under his chin, a tub of ice cream under his left arm, a bottle of chocolate syrup in his left hand, and a plastic grocery bag in his right hand. He was clearly struggling but it was much more entertaining for Genie to watch him than to help. He had also changed into more comfortable clothes. He was wearing gray, school sweatpants that had "Blakeridge Dive Team" written on the side. Diving and swimming were the only sports he participated in. He said anything else was stupid and he always came up with a reason he didn't play. Genie always knew that it was because he wasn't any good at the others. He also had a plain white t-shirt on and it was little on the snug side but Genie didn't mind at all. She glanced over in his direction just as the tub of ice cream was slipping from under his arm. She jumped up and rushed to where he was standing by the fridge.

"The ice cream!"

She squealed just as she caught it from falling to the ground. She held it and looked up at him.

"Would you like some help, Mr. Independent?"

He chuckled and looked straight through her sarcastic expression and replied, "Sure, could you scoop the ice cream into two of the glasses."

Genie nodded and made her way over to the farthest cabinet. She knew exactly where his glasses were. Tyler had three of the old fashion ice cream/shake glasses and he only used them for movie night. As Genie reached for two of the glasses, it felt weird for there to be only two being used tonight. It was always three. Genie looked down and paused.

Tyler sauntered over to her, "Something wrong?"

She shook her head in silence then grabbed the glasses.

She exhaled but when she looked up, Tyler was staring right at her.

"Something's wrong. C'mon let's talk," Tyler said putting his arm around her.

Tyler had a twin sister and his best friend was Genie, he knew exactly how to deal with women. He had his arms around her and she laid her head on his shoulder like a little girl.

She smiled.

"I'm fine Ty Ty, I really am. It's just weird without Addie here."

Tyler gave her a squeeze and looked straight into Genie's blue eyes.

"I don't mind it one bit."

Genie felt her stomach flip. Her heart was racing and Tyler looked at her and began to lean in. Genie tried to seem calm and she leaned too. When their lips met, she closed her eyes and her insides melted. It was like hot fudge running down the interior of the ice cream glass. It was perfect. Tyler's hand brushed against her cheek. It was about five seconds before Genie pulled back. Tyler's eyes slowly opened. Genie stared at him in awe. She had kissed guys before but never Tyler, definitely not Tyler. Tyler grabbed the glasses that were dangling from Genie's hands. Genie's heart flipped whenever their hands touched. She didn't like Tyler, not like that at least. She never had a crush on him and she wasn't about to start now. What if they started dating? What would that do to their friendship? And what about that kiss? Would she tell Addie? Would Tyler bring it up? Had he planned that? What about Lindsey? Were they going to break up? Genie just stood there staring at the tile.

Tyler was on the futon with two glasses of ice cream, "You coming?"

Genie shook her head to make all the questions go away.

"I'll be right back," Genie said turning away from the couch and Tyler and towards the small hallway that led back to Tyler's bedroom and bathroom. She turned left into the bathroom and shut the door behind her. When she looked in the mirror, she didn't recognize the person who stared back. This other person's cheeks were red and their blue eyes danced with excitement. Her hair was messy. She couldn't let Tyler see her like this. She splashed water on her face. She needed a brush. She turned from the mirror and searched for a brush in the wreckage that was the small bathroom. What was she doing? This wasn't Addie's bathroom. It was Tyler's. She wasn't going to find a brush in here. She pushed the toilet seat down and sat for a moment. She needed to collect herself. She glanced around the bathroom. Until now, she hadn't noticed how dirty it was. There were two towels just lying on the tile. A pair of jeans rested on the bathtub's ledge. Inside those jeans was a pair of plaid boxers. An old T-shirt was half in the small trashcan and half draped over the side. The shampoo bottles on the bathtub's ledge were knocked unto their sides and were dripping a neon blue substance all over the tub and floor. She stood and looked in the mirror again and realized that she looked more like herself now. She opened the bathroom door and sauntered out. Tyler's eyes followed her movement and she plopped down next to him on the couch. He handed her a glass. He had the remote in the other hand. He pressed the play button and the movie began. Tyler brought a spoonful of ice cream to his mouth. Genie glanced over at him and smiled. The movie played and right on cue, Genie started to cry when John Cusak held the boom box outside the window.

Tyler looked over at her and laughed, "Awww, Gen, come here."

Tyler held his arms open and Genie fell right into them. She laid her head on his chest and he smiled. He slipped his arms around her. She felt his strong muscles around her and she felt protected. She let herself relax and soon she began to feel tired. Tyler leaned back and she let her body follow his. The two fell asleep on the couch and when Addie came busting through the door, she saw Tyler with his arms around her friend and Genie was cuddled up beside her brother. Addie was stunned and cleared her throat. When they didn't wake up, Addie stomped to the other side of the couch. She stood over Tyler and hit him with her purse.

"Whoa, whoa. Hey! Stop! Addie, I'm awake, we're awake."

Genie slowly opened her eyes. She stretched out on the couch and felt her muscles tighten. Addie stood over the couch with her hands on her hips.

"Does someone wanna tell me what's going on here?"

Addie asked walking to the other side of the couch where Genie lay.

"You. Come with me. We need to talk."

Addie grabbed Genie's wrist and pulled her off of the couch and down the hallway. Genie stumbled after her and when she looked back to where Tyler was he was rubbing his eyes and beginning to stand. Addie released her grip on Genie's arm when they were inside Tyler's room. Genie walked over to where the bed was and fell back on the hunter green comforter. Tyler's room smelled just as his car did, Axe and Mountain Dew. Only this time there was the scent of sweat, as well, which ruined the other two odors. Addie closed and locked the door before coming over to sit next to Genie. When Addie had woken them up, Genie had sensed anger but when Addie turned to look at her when they sat next to each other on his bed, Addie's expression wasn't of anger but of excitement. Genie rolled her shoulders back and exhaled. Thank goodness that she wasn't mad.

"So, how was your date?"

When Genie had asked this, Addie almost burst with excitement.

"It was great. The movie was great. The food was great. Aidan was great. I mean, he was just so charming. He wasn't pressuring or anything, just sweet."

"I am so happy to hear that. When are you guys going out again?"

Addie shrugged and looked away.

"Oh I don't know . . . tomorrow night."

Genie was stunned. For Aidan to want to go out with Addie the very next day meant that he must really like her. Genie could feel her jaw drop and Addie noticed immediately what Genie was thinking.

Addie continued, "So can you come over tomorrow around five so we can talk about it. He's taking me to lunch and probably a walk."

Genie almost answered before she remembered, "I would love to but Trinity is going be at home for the next week. She's getting in some time tomorrow. I'm not even going to be around whenever she gets to the house."

Addie cringed and replied, "Wait where are you going to be? Is it something for the Gazette?"

Genie shook her head.

"No, I volunteered so that I wouldn't be around."

"You could always come here and hide in Tyler's arms. What was that all about?"

It was absolutely amazing how quickly Addie could turn the conversation around and start the interrogation.

"It was nothing. I was cold and tired and we fell asleep. Nothing more happened."

Addie raised her eyebrow and tried to analyze what Genie had just said.

"Are you sure? I'm gonna talk to Ty about this later," Addie said.

"Okay. Nothing happened."

Genie got up and unlocked the door. She turned before opening it.

"Text me about your date tomorrow. I'll be listening to Trinity talk about how great college is."

Genie opened the door and started down the hallway before Addie called after her, "Tell your sister I said hi. Oh and how much I miss her. Ha-Ha. Bye!"

Genie laughed.

Trinity had always hated Addie. She never gave a reason but every time that Addie came to the house, Trinity would roll her eyes and make up an excuse to leave. Genie waved goodbye to Tyler before walking out the door to the apartment. She skipped down the stairs that led up to Tyler's place. When her feet hit the cold ground, she suddenly remembered that she didn't have her car. She didn't need it though because she lived across the block from the Moore's. Genie walked along the street. She walked in the middle of the street but whenever she checked her phone to see what time it was, she knew no cars would be driving through this neighborhood at 11 o'clock at night. This was the nicer part of town and no one would be driving their BMW or Mercedes around at this time of night. She checked her phone again just to fidget. It was 11:11. She closed her eyes and made a wish quickly. She couldn't believe what she automatically wished for. She followed the road until it came to a dead end after the last house on that street. The Chesapeake Bay's waters tossed in the cool night air. For a moment, Genie stood with one arm on top of a wooden peg and the other gripping the old and worn rope that was strung between the wooden pegs. The sound of the waves calmed her. Living on the Chesapeake Bay had its bright sides. The beautiful sun rises in the summer that reflected off the water made for excellent post cards, the crabbing was the town's livelihood, and the fact that her town was a part of what made Maryland unique, the Bay. She soaked in the scent of the water before turning right and continuing to walk home. She headed onto a path that was paved so that kids could walk to school. She followed the path that was parallel to the cliff that overlooked the water. She walked about five minutes on the path before the path came to a street.

Her street had about twenty houses on it. There were ten on each side. Each house was two stories and had shutters and a white picket fence. Her house was a light yellow and had blue shutters. The grass was dry and hard because the lawn was not at its finest in March. The winter had done its damage. Genie walked up her house's two steps that led to the porch. She opened the door and let the warmth of the house envelop her before she noticed her grandfather sitting in his recliner. Poppy loved that recliner. It was probably thirty years old and it had scratches all over its brown surface. He looked up when she closed the front door behind her.

"Poppy, I didn't see you there."

Her grandfather smiled. He was the type of man that everyone thought of when they thought of a grandpa. He was a little old man who was around 70 years old. He liked to wear a brown sweater and light brown corduroy pants. He had reading glasses and he always wore brown dress shoes. He had white hair and his eyes were a warm brown. He had wrinkles but for his age, he didn't look all that bad. He lived with Genie's mom because after Victor died, Ellen was a wreck and someone needed to care for her children while she grieved. So, Ellen's father moved in and it was better for both Ellen and Poppy.

"Where were you, my dear?"

Genie's grandfather asked, with not a bit of worry or concern in his voice. It was most likely because he already knew the answer.

"I was over at Addie's."

"And Tyler's. Tyler is such a nice young man. He's coming over to help Noah tomorrow with the ah . . . oh what's it called . . . the, uh, pine box derby."

Genie smiled.

"I'm not going to be here tomorrow during the day. I'm going to the soup kitchen to help prepare for the dinner rush."

"Don't you want to be home when Trinity gets here? She's eager to see you. I'm sure she'll want to spend sometime with you."

Genie felt her insides go to flames. Trinity hated her and she hated Trinity. No one wanted to spend time with each other but Poppy didn't know that.

"I'll find another time to spend with her."

Poppy nodded and returned to reading the newspaper. The only newspaper that he read was the <u>Deal Island Gazette</u>. It was a small paper but it took him all week to read because he read two articles a day. It was his way of showing his support for Genie and her dreams of writing.

Genie climbed the stairs and stopped at the first door on the right. Her room looked eerily empty and lifeless in the dark. Genie didn't even bother to turn on the light or change into pajamas. Instead, she climbed into bed and shut her eyes. Her last thought before she drifted off to sleep was about Tyler. This wasn't the first time that he appeared in one of her dreams.

Chapter 4

Genie sighed as she slid into her car and shut the door. It was 4:42 and the time for her to leave couldn't have come any sooner. She had spent the day at the soup kitchen, helping them cook and organize, and clean up. It was the kind of work that made you exhausted even if you only worked for an hour. Genie had arrived at the beaten up old warehouse at 11 o'clock this morning. When she saw that a friend of hers from middle school was there to help as well, she relaxed and thought that maybe it wouldn't be so bad after all. Bailey had made the day a little better too. Genie and Bailey had talked for hours about what they'd been doing since eighth grade graduation. Bailey had become interested in art and was very passionate about abstract pieces. Bailey had done her best to describe what kind of painting and sketches she did but it must have been obvious that Genie did not understand because Bailey gave up trying to explain. Bailey had also mentioned an art exhibition in the next town over that coming Thursday. Genie really wasn't all that interested in attending but tried not to let it show. Genie had talked about her work with the gazette and how she wanted to be a journalist. Bailey had been a good listener and asked reasonable questions. When the time had come that the work they were assigned to do would not allow them to socialize anymore, the girls separated and no longer spoke. Now, Genie sat in her car and let the cold air dry the sweat that she had worked up doing the different projects around the soup kitchen. She turned the key and started the engine. Right as she was about to pull out of her parking space, her phone beeped. She reached onto the passenger seat and picked up the phone. She had one new text message. She pressed the center button, allowing the message to open. It read,

Hey! Just got baq from my date with Aidan. Can't wait to tell u about it. Call me wen u r baq from the soup kitchen. L8r luv

Genie threw the phone back onto the seat and again, took grip of the wheel. She pulled out of the parking lot and turned onto the main road. She watched as the scenery passed. The water looked much brighter today than it had the night before. She knew that the water must have been freezing because her car told her that the air outside the car was cold which meant the water was absolutely freezing. The thought of how cold the water was made her shiver. She turned again, only this time it was onto the main street that was the heart of Deal Island. Main Street cut right through downtown. This was where all the restaurants, coffee shops, tourist shops, and doctors' offices were. It was also where the Gazette's headquarters were. She found a spot outside of Blake's Brews.

Isaac Blake was the richest man in town whenever Deal Island was becoming established. Of course, Mr. Blake bought numerous businesses and even started his own school(Blakeridge Academy). He liked to invest his wealth in things that never change. Children will always need to be educated, that'll never change. Many businesses around town had the name Blake worked into them somehow or another. Though he was not the founder of Deal Island, he is the face that all of the residents put to the founding of the town.

Blake's Brews was a coffee shop and bookstore that Genie had always found enchanting. Inside the street level shop were classic novels, recliners, leather couches, lit candles, and of course the coffee counter in the front. The shop was covered in wood. It wasn't outdated looking but it had an older feel to it. Genie had always found the little shop to be extremely charming and even before she had heard of the novels that were shelved in the back of the store, she wanted to read them. She began to drink coffee the year before with the soul purpose that she wanted to relax in the shop. She couldn't do so without buying something so she began to drink coffee.

To get to the gazette's headquarters, you had to walk to the back of the coffee shop, where there would be a door hidden by two monstrous bookshelves. Behind that door was a staircase, and once you have climbed that staircase, you were inside the newspaper's office. The office was nothing fancy. The floor was covered in a gray carpet and there were four desks in the main room. There were always people at two of the desks and on the other two were stacks of papers, newspapers, printer paper, and sticky notes, anything that you could imagine in an office.

Margaret was the secretary for the newspaper. She was in her late 50's early 60's. She was a heavier set woman who had a pudgy face and curly gray hair. She always had a cotton dress with a floral pattern and the color of her heels varied depending on the type of flower that was on her dress. If Genie didn't know her better, she'd have guessed that Margaret was one of those crazy, old, cat-ladies that almost every neighborhood had. Margaret usually didn't have a lot to do but she was there so that whenever there was something to do, Arnold didn't have to do it. Arnold was the boss/manager of the paper. He was editor and he also made sure the paper got printed in time. Arnold had his own office, which was just a room that was off to the side. When Genie entered into the office, Margaret looked up from her game of Internet solitaire. Today's dress was purple flowers and to match, she had white closed toed heels.

"Hi, Ms. Margaret. Does Arnold have time to talk?"

Margaret leaned over her desk and peered into Arnold's office.

"It doesn't look like he's on the phone. Go ahead in."

Margaret smiled warmly before sitting back down in her chair and clicking another card. Genie walked to the back of the large room where the door to Arnold's office was wide open. Arnold was sitting at his desk staring at the screen of his old and outdated computer.

"Hello Genesis," he said looking up from the glowing screen, "I usually don't see you around here on Saturdays. What can I do for you?"

Arnold wasn't a mean man. He wasn't a nice one either. He was just very passionate about the paper. He didn't have much of a life Outside the Gazette so he spent most of his time worrying about the paper. Because the newspaper wasn't a huge moneymaker or a dream job of any sort, he was the perfect man for the job. Genie looked at the wrinkles on Arnold's face. It made her kind of sad. He was only around 45 and he had more wrinkles than Margaret did. He used to have a wife and two kids. He had been a great father but his wife was just awful. Arnold used to be close friends with Genie's dad. Victor had been there for Arnold when his wife left. Victor was almost like an older brother even though they were around the same age. When Victor died, it seemed as though everything that Arnold had to live for was gone and he began to live in a world all by himself. He was usually stressed about something but other than anxiety, Genie had never seen him express another emotion.

He sat with his polo buttoned all the way up, staring at Genie.

"I just didn't think that I would come on Monday. I thought that I'd pick up my topic for the week now instead," she said looking straight at him.

"Oh," he answered surprised, "great. I have it right . . . here."

He picked up a piece of paper that looked more like a flyer than it did a topic.

"I actually want to give you this," he said handing her the paper. "It's a writing competition that's hosted by the University of Maryland," Arnold continued, "It would look great on college applications if you do well in it."

Genie studied the paper. She skimmed it and noticed that the due date wasn't for another month or so.

"Thank you, I really appreciate it. I'll get started on this. I'll be back on Monday for my topic then."

"No, you don't need to come back on Monday. If you come on Wednesday, I'll tell you about where you'll be going."

Genie nodded and turned to leave. She folded the paper and slid it into her back pocket. As she headed down the stairs, back down to the coffee shop, she thought about the competition.

It said that the topic that you were supposed to write about was a question. They didn't give a question though. The paper had said that they were looking for the applicant to make up a question that fascinated or concerned them. As Genie drove back to her house, she thought about the things that she questioned in her life. She thought about her dad's death and if that had raised any questions in her mind. She was so young when it happened, that she couldn't really think of anything that she had questioned. Her mother's sanity maybe, but that wasn't writing competition material.

She was turning onto her street when she recognized her sister's car. Trinity's little black compact was parallel parked in front of the mailbox.

Good thing we aren't expecting mail today, Genie thought, good parking sis.

There was smoke rising from the chimney. They only lit fires in the chimney on Christmas and snow days. It must be lit to make Trinity feel at home. Great.

Genie stepped out of her car and slammed the door shut. She opened the gate to the fence and shut it behind her. She stepped up on the porch and opened the front door. Trinity was sitting in the chair that faced the door, so her flawless face was the first thing Genie saw when she walked in.

"Genesis! You're home! Were you at the Moore's house again?"

Her mother asked as though she hadn't been home for days. Ellen turned to Trinity and said; "You know how she's always over there."

Ellen said it to Trinity like she had said 'Noah's having difficulty potty training' to one of her book club friends. Genie was baffled at her mom's comment.

Trinity returned her glare over to Genie, "That reminds me. How is your friend Mady?"

Genie rolled her eyes. Her sister was trying to forget about Addie and how one time, one of Trinity's boyfriends got caught making out with Addie.

"Oh, you mean Addie? She's good. Also, I wasn't at her house. I was at the soup kitchen volunteering." Trinity and Ellen looked at each other in astonishment.

"Well, Genesis, that is just lovely." Ellen muttered the words as though she was out of breath.

Ellen continued, "Trinity here was just talking about how she is doing this program with children. She, correct me if I'm wrong Trinity, works with children who have mental disabilities and are in less fortunate housing."

Genie could feel her insides tear. Genie had just spent the day at a soup kitchen and her sister had already one-upped her, children with disabilities who didn't have money. It doesn't get any better than that. They might as well give her the Nobel Peace Prize now.

Trinity nodded when her mother had finished. Genie didn't even want to attempt to stay a part of the conversation. Trinity called for her as Genie climbed the stairs.

"Hey, Genie, I'll see you later. I really want to sit down with you so that we may have a good talk. You know, just sisters."

Genie nodded an artificial nod. If Trinity ever acted like a real sister, Genie probably wouldn't hate her so much.

Chapter 5

Genie stood at the steps of the Blakeridge Academy, facing her sister.

"If you do anything that embarrasses me or any of my friends, I swear, I will tell mom some of the ugly things that you did when you were my age."

Trinity sighed and looked back at Genie.

"You are such a liar. I didn't do anything wrong when I was here."

Genie raised an eyebrow.

"Doesn't mean I can't make stuff up."

Trinity chuckled, "And you actually think mom would believe you?"

With that, Trinity pushed past Genie and walked in the front doors of the building. Having Trinity visit her old high school for the day was just about the worst idea Genie could ever imagine. When Ellen had said that she'd called the school and made sure it was okay, last night at dinner, Genie almost spit out her lasagna. Trinity, of course, was giddy with excitement. Now, Trinity was marching full speed into the front office in her silver heels and dark denim skinny jeans. Her black blazer made the casual outfit more sophisticated. Genie waited a few moments before turning away from the front door. She didn't want to be anywhere near her sister today. As she turned, she noticed Tyler walking towards the school from the student parking lot. Genie quickly skipped down the steps and ran to him. Tyler didn't notice her until after she was five feet away from him and approaching quickly. He quickly held out his arms and Genie rushed into them. She held him tight and felt his arms wrap around her.

"Good morning," he said letting go.

She took a step away from him so that she could walk with him.

"No, it's not good at all. Trinity is here . . . at Blakeridge . . . today . . . here."

He squinted and looked away as if he had just smelled something completely rotten.

"Why is she here," he asked, "Didn't she graduate last year? I thought that we'd never have to see her here again."

Genie laughed. She knew that he disliked her just as much as she did. Trinity seemed great from the outside but when you were an insider, all you wanted was to throw her out of the circle.

"I don't know why she's here either. My mom said it had something to do with her wanting to be a teacher and wanting to see her old teachers again," Genie said walking up the steps for a second time.

Tyler replied, "Are we sure that they want to see her again?"

Genie shook her head, "Tyler, I think we're alone on the whole hating her thing. I think everyone else thinks she's an angel that we are just blessed to have in our lives."

Tyler fake gagged and held the door open as Genie entered the crowded hallway. Inside, Tyler and Genie walked past the office. Through the glass window, they saw Trinity giving the vice principal a hug. Genie sighed and Tyler gave her a nudge as they continued to walk.

"Hey, at least you get your topic today."

Tyler was referring to her piece in the newspaper but even that couldn't cheer Genie up.

"Actually, I don't have to go after school today. I only have to go on Wednesday this week."

Tyler raised his eyebrows as if to say, 'really'. He looked away then looked back at Genie.

"Hey, why don't I save you from that monster tonight. We'll escape and do something. I'll buy coffee if you want."

Genie laughed out loud a little. The thought of sitting in Blake's Brews with Tyler made her feel kind of warm inside. It would be saving her from an afternoon with Trinity. She'd rather spend a day in a Turkish prison then spend an afternoon with Trinity.

Genie nodded and waved goodbye to Tyler. Her locker was here and his was not. He walked away, backpack hanging from his muscular shoulders, his hands in the pockets of his khaki pants. Maybe this day wouldn't be so bad after all.

Genie looked in the mirror that she had on the inside of her locker. Her navy blue vest looked worse than it ever had. Her plaid uniform skirt seemed a little longer than it had before. Had she shrunk? Whatever. Her blonde hair was straight and her makeup looked good. She reached down to pick up her bag when she noticed the sparkly ribbon tied to the handle. Tyler had given her the sparkly ribbon last year. He said he found it and when he saw that it was sparkly it made him think of her, so he gave it to her. Of all the colorful ribbons tied to the handle., that one was her favorite. She picked up her bag and headed to her first class. The wood floors of the school looked particularly shiny today, as did the lockers. Maybe a group of students got in trouble and had to come in over the weekend and clean the school.

She shrugged off the thought before heading into a classroom. Inside, 14 students sat with their heads on the desk, or talking to the person next to them. No one was a fan of Monday mornings. Genie took her seat in between two of her least favorite people, Lindsey Davis and Michelle Parker. Lindsey acknowledged that Genie was there by giving her a fake smile and nodding. Michelle on the other hand, was a lot like Lindsey in the IQ department. And let me tell you, between the two of them, it wasn't a large department at all. Michelle sat examining her long, red nails. Genie slid down in her seat and waited for the announcements to come over the intercom. No one ever listened to the announcements unless the words, "free" or "food" were mentioned. Usually, the vice principal did the announcements but whenever a young, female voice came over the intercom, Genie knew exactly whom it was.

"Good Morning, Blakeridge Academy. It is Monday, March 11. I am pleased to bring you the morning announcements today. Obviously, this is not Mrs. Sims. Mrs. Sims, your wonderful vice principal, has let me, Trinity Anderson, do the morning announcements this fabulous winter morning."

Genie wanted to kill Trinity and had she been at arms length, she probably would have.

"Okay so, today there will be a freshmen book club meeting after school. Also, Varsity boys' hockey has practice at eight o'clock tonight. Oh, and last but not least, the Equestrian team will be meeting by the stables today. Thank you and have a wonderful day."

Click.

The announcements were over but the humiliation was not.

Lindsey cackled and looked over at Genie, "Have a wonderful day."

Lindsey mocked Trinity. Genie didn't blame her. If Lindsey had an older sister that did the same thing, Genie would have spent all day mocking her. It just sucked that it was Trinity.

Genie's History teacher, Mrs. Jenkins, stood from her seat and looked at Genie, "My-my, your sister was such an incredible student. She sounds as though she is doing well. How has she been?"

More than anything, Genie wanted to yell, "well with the way things are going now, she'll be canonized a saint by May."

Genie controlled herself enough to mutter, "Fine, she's been doing very well at Maryland."

Mrs. Jenkins smiled warmly and replied, "I knew she would."

Inside, Genie thought, we all knew she would. You could meet her for three minutes in an elevator and you would know she's doing well.

The bell rang and class began.

World History couldn't have been more boring. The entire class period, Genie stared at the giant mole that was on the back of Mrs. Jenkin's neck. It had a single hair growing from the center of it. She should have that looked at.

When class ended, Genie stood and held her bag. She waited until most of the students had cleared the hallway before she made her way through the rushing students. She already had the books she needed so there wasn't a need to stop at her locker. As she walked through the crowd of look-alikes, she noticed a new face. Because he was moving so fast, she couldn't see him but she knew that if there was a new kid, she wasn't having the worst day in the world. He was.

As she walked through the hallway, she noticed a blonde that wasn't in uniform. Genie quickly stopped, not even caring that she would be late for class. She stomped up in front of Trinity. Trinity was smiling brightly which only made Genie angrier.

"How could you?!"

Trinity seemed surprised by what Genie said but Genie didn't lighten up.

"I asked you to not embarrass me and what did you do? You broadcast it all over the school. Thanks so much. You are the best sister in the world."

Genie turned on her topsiders and stomped away. Trinity gasped then turned in the opposite direction. Even though Genie was probably 40 feet away from her sister, she could hear the clicking and clacking of her awful heels hitting the wood floor. Genie sped up her pace whenever the bell rang. She turned the corner and ran into a senior who was casually strolling through the hall. She ran into him with such force that she fell to the ground with a thump. Genie didn't recognize who it was until he was reaching down offering her a hand. Aidan Campbell was leaning over with his hand outreached.

"I am so sorry. I was just running away from my sister."

As childish as it sounded, it was the truth and she knew that Aidan would understand.

"Yeah, Addie told me about that. She said that Trinity wasn't a huge fan of her," Aidan said pulling Genie to her feet.

Aidan's voice was very deep but not in an old man or intimidating way. Instead it sounded gentle and kind.

"Ha ha, yeah, Addie and my sister were never best friends."

Aidan laughed and picked up one of Genie's books that had fallen out of her bag in the collision.

"Well, I better go," Aidan, said walking away.

Now Genie was really late to class. When she opened the door to the room, her Spanish teacher, Mr. Lander, was leaning on his desk talking. He stopped whenever Genie entered the room.

"And why are we late Ms. Anderson?"

Genie was out of breath and at a loss for words. Her knight in shining armor came to her rescue.

"Mr. Lander, sir, uh Genie had asked me to help Trinity find the principal and I didn't help her, which is why she's late sir. She was helping her sister. I knew where the principal was and I didn't say anything so Genie had to go and find him herself."

Genie watched in amazement and gratitude as Tyler made this all up. Tyler looked at her and gave her a wink at the end. Mr. Lander looked at Genie and then at Tyler and rolled his eyes.

"Is this true?"

Genie nodded and stood as the class watched the scene unfold.

"Find your seat."

Genie swiveled around the desks and sat in her seat. She threw her bag down beside her and leaned back in her wooden chair. Thank God for Tyler.

Chapter 6

"What was that all about," Tyler asked as he drove out of the school parking lot.

"What do you mean?"

Genie asked looking at him from the passenger seat of his truck.

"I mean, why were you late today."

"What are you my mother?"

Tyler chuckled.

"Last time I checked no but I don't know how many more lies I can make up on the spot like that."

Genie smiled and smacked his thigh.

"Thanks again for that. I was really late because of Trinity. I had to talk to her about the morning announcements thing."

Tyler winced at her words.

He replied, "Yeah that was a little on the rough side. Whenever I heard that on the intercom, I just knew that you were mortified."

"Yeah. I was. I really don't see a reason to forgive her though so my plan is to hold it against her until I visit her grave."

Tyler laughed as he turned the wheel and steered the car onto Main Street.

"Alrighty, then."

Genie watched as he pulled up in front of Blake's. The scent of cinnamon filled the air, which meant that there were fresh rolls inside Blake's. Tyler followed Genie as she stepped up onto the curb and walked around the tree that was set near the curb on the sidewalk. Genie pulled the door open and as she stepped in, the warmth enveloped her. The overwhelming scents of cinnamon, coffee, and old books rushed to her. Tyler followed her in, letting the last burst of cold air enter. Genie went and sat down in one of the love seats. Tyler looked toward her.

"Cinnamon spice latte, right?"

"Oh yeah, thanks, Camo."

Tyler nodded as he turned toward the counter. Genie watched him as he ordered at the counter. He turned around after the cashier went to make his order. A few moments later, the cashier in the red apron returned holding two mugs. Tyler handed him the cash and the guy in the apron handed him the mugs. Tyler turned with a mug in each hand. Genie reached out and took the red mug from him. She held it under her nose and let the steam rise from the latte. The scent was perfect and she couldn't have been any happier than she was at that very moment. Tyler took a seat next to her and he let out a long breath as he leaned back in the chair. Genie smiled and took a sip.

He reached his mug towards her, "Cheers?"

"To what," she asked.

"To," he replied, "A relaxing afternoon away from your devilish sister."

Genie laughed and let her mug clink against his. It was something to cheer.

If only her sister was taken to a mental institution where she belonged, Genie would do more than cheer. She'd have a parade and Tyler would lead it through town.

She brought the mug back to her lips and let herself drink the steaming liquid. Tyler put his mug down and rose from the seat.

"Where are you going?"

Genie asked, putting hers down as well.

"I want to show you something. I'll be back in just a minute. Give me one-second."

Genie watched as he stepped up onto the platform that elevated the bookshelves in the back part of the shop. Genie leaned back in the chair and watched as the people outside the shop passed. There were so many people she knew that passed but from inside the shop they looked like strangers in another world. Two women in jogging gear, a man with a briefcase, a woman pushing a stroller, a child walking a small lapdog, and an elderly couple holding hands. Just as the two older people passed, Tyler came and sat down next to Genie.

"Close your eyes."

"Why," she insisted.

"Because, it's part of the fun and I never have surprises so let me do it my way."

"Fine, fine, fine."

Genie closed her eyes and listened to the sound of a large book hitting the table in front of them. Then came the sounds of pages turning.

Then the sound of Tyler's voice, "And . . . open."

Genie's eyes flew open and she gasped when she saw what was in front of her. On the table was an old pop-up book. It must have been brought to the bookshop in the 60's because it was dusty and the way it was put together was definitely old fashioned. Though it was older, it was brightly colored and the images seemed to dance not only on the page but also off of the book's surface and in Genie's heart.

She glanced at Tyler and he sat watching her, biting his bottom lip.

Genie finally spoke, "Where did you find this?"

Tyler chuckled and flipped the page.

"Believe it or not, your dad had showed me this."

Genie couldn't believe Tyler's words. Her father? Tyler must have been really young when this happened.

"When?" Genie found herself asking.

Tyler adjusted himself on the couch before continuing.

"When I was in sixth grade, I came over to your house to talk with you about a project or something like that. I remember it was only like the second time I had ever met him. You had told me he was sick but he was just so happy. I couldn't believe that he was dying from cancer. Anyway, you weren't home and I was getting ready to leave when he stopped me. He said that he wanted me to have something. I thought that maybe it was something that I had forgotten the last time I was there. A couple minutes later, he came up and in his hand was this," Tyler pointed to the book that Genie was now flipping through.

Tyler continued, "He said that you didn't like this type of stuff and that Noah wouldn't understand. When I asked him why me, he said that he saw a lot of potential in me and that he knew that I'd be around for a while."

Genie couldn't fathom all that Tyler had just revealed. Why wouldn't she have liked it? In sixth grade, her father was only home for three weeks before he went back to the hospital where he eventually died. Why Tyler? In the sixth grade, they had only been friends for a couple months. That made no sense. Tyler cleared his throat, waiting for a response. Many questions ran through her mind so she picked one.

"How did it end up here?"

With the way Tyler's answers had been for the past couple of questions, the only thing that would have surprised her more would be if he said that Victor had flown from heaven and delivered it himself while riding on a unicorn.

Tyler answered, "Well after your father passed, I felt bad about keeping it. It felt wrong. So I talked to Mr. Hansen and only being 11, I really didn't see the importance in keeping it. So I donated it to the shop and here it is."

Genie ran her fingers over one of the pop up characters. The one that Genie was admiring was a tropical bird that was elevated from the page. In a fancy script, was written the words "And colorful as he was, he never let anyone see his true colors." Tyler ran his fingers over Genie's.

"This page is my favorite."

Genie nodded at Tyler's comment. She hadn't seen everything in the book but she already knew it was hers too. Tyler flipped the page over Genie's fingers and she quickly took them out of their old position. The next page had a tiger bursting from the page. The colors were vibrant even though the cover was beaten around and a faded brown. Tyler sat with Genie and flipped through the pages for over an hour. They went through over three cups of hot chocolate, and two lattes each. They sat in silence but the way Tyler was so patient with Genie said so much more than words could ever describe. Genie was overwhelmed with thoughts of her father when her cell phone began to ring. The loud ringing brought her and Tyler both back to reality.

"Hello," Genie said pressing the phone to her ear, "mom, calm down. I'm with Tyler. Yes, he's gonna bring me to back to Blakeridge to get my car. Okay, bye."

Tyler squinted one dark brown eye, "She mad?"

Genie shook her head. She picked up her purse while standing up. As she stood, Genie suddenly realized that she was still in her uniform. Tyler then stood beside her. His eyes dashed around the littered table. He quickly grabbed the pop up book from the table and brought it to the counter.

"Put this away for me. Thanks."

Genie was already halfway out the door when Tyler ran back to the couch for his coat.

"Tips on the table!" Tyler called as he ran towards for the door.

Genie stood outside the truck waiting for Tyler. He rushed out the door and hit the unlock button. Genie gripped the chrome handle and pulled the door open. She threw her purse in and gripped the seat as she tried to hoist herself onto the seat. Tyler had walked halfway to the driver's side when he realized what difficulty Genie was having. He turned and rushed to her aid. He grabbed her waist and pushed her up to the seat.

Genie looked down to him and smiled, "Thanks."

Genie giggled as Tyler rushed around the front of the truck. For the first time since she left the coffee shop, she took notice how cold it was. She glanced down at her exposed arm. She ran her fingers over the goose bumps on her arm. Tyler opened the door to the truck and jumped in.

"Whooo. It is pretty chilly out there."

He said as he jammed his keys into the ignition. Genie watched him and took notice of the way he looked. He didn't put his jacket on before rushing out of the shop so his skin was a little red. His cheeks were flushed and whenever he looked over to her, she noticed how obvious his dimples were. Genie started to laugh and he looked over as the car turned off of Main Street.

"What is up with you today," he asked reaching over and tapping her leg.

She tried her hardest not to laugh any more but the giggles flooded out. Soon Tyler began to chuckle and before either of them knew it, they were both laughing uncontrollably. Tyler managed to keep control of his truck long enough to pull into the school parking lot. Genie breathed as steadily as she could. She watched, as Tyler pulled up next to her car in the empty parking lot. The school looked different in the dark when no one was there. Tyler pushed open his door and jumped out. He grabbed her bag from the backseat. Genie grabbed her purse and slid out of his truck. Genie shoved her key in the lock and turned it to the right. She pulled open the driver's door and took her bag from Tyler. When she turned around, she didn't have any time to think before Tyler grabbed her waist and pulled her close. Genie watched as her breath rose from her open mouth and looked like smoke as it drifted away. He pulled her in and began to kiss her. Genie could feel her knees going weak. She could no longer feel the cold, only Tyler's heat and the joy that he brought her. He breathed in and Genie exhaled. Finally, he released his grip of her. She stumbled back. He chuckled and turned away to go to his car. He looked back at her and smiled. Genie couldn't help but notice how innocent he looked and how odd she felt. He looked like a little boy who had just heard that he got to stay up late. She slipped into her car and she sat and stared at the steering wheel until after she was sure Tyler's red pick up was nowhere in sight. Then she leaned back in her seat and screamed but not a short squeal, more of a roller coaster drop scream. The way that little children scream when they see Santa Claus. At that moment, Genie knew that she couldn't imagine being happier than she was at that very moment in a cold car, in the middle of an empty parking lot, in the middle of the evening.

Chapter 7

Genie stood waiting outside Arnold's office. Margaret had said that he was on a "very important conference call." Arnold was never doing anything important except for sending an email with articles for this Sunday's paper to the publisher. That was just about as important as it came for the small newspaper. Genie was growing impatient. She had come straight from school and her blue tights were bothering her. She really didn't want to go home to another rant from Trinity. After Genie had come home from her evening with Tyler on Monday, Trinity had questioned her on every detail of the night. Of course, Genie wasn't stupid enough to tell Trinity about the ending but she did tell her about their father's book and how he had given it to Tyler, and what he said to him. Trinity was outraged that Victor hadn't given it to one of his own children. Genie had tried to explain that it was a young boy's book and not a little girl's story but Trinity refused to understand her father's logic.

Genie mentioned what had stuck out the most to her, "Tyler said that dad had said the reason he gave the book to him was because he knew that Tyler would be around for a while. What do you think that means, Trinity?"

When Genie asked, her sister shrugged and pulled out her cell phone. She pretended to act busy on it. She was never busy with anything important.

"Maybe dad thought that you and Tyler would get married or something. I don't know. You have to remember that dad was very sick back then."

Genie nodded, understanding what her sister was trying to say. It was too late, it had gotten Genie thinking. Were her and Tyler meant to be together? What would Addie think? What would her mother and Poppy think? Would Noah be happy with his best friend and sister dating? Does Tyler even want to go out with her or were the kisses just a spur of the moment act? What about Lindsey? Did Tyler love Lindsey? What does love even mean? Tyler said he loved her all the time. What did he mean? Did he mean like a sister or like . . . ?

Arnold knocked on the wall and Genie was brought back to reality. He stood in his usual weekday attire. A pinstripe shirt, khaki pants, and a simple solid colored tie.

"Hi, um, I'm here for my topic."

Arnold nodded and headed back into his small office. Genie turned and stood in the doorway and watched as Arnold rummaged through his desk. When he emerged from his office he held a map. Genie's hope died. When Arnold had a map that meant that she had to go somewhere to write about a nearby town's event. She wasn't in the mood this week to drive around and waste her gas on some stupid elementary school play or sports game. When Arnold handed her the paper, Genie looked for the name of the event. When she found the name of it on the top portion of the paper, she was very disappointed. Tomorrow, after school, she had to attend the Chesapeake Art Exhibition. It was about half an hour away and it started at seven. The only up side to having to travel to her writing piece was that Genie would get that much more time away from Trinity.

"Thanks Mr. Arnold. I'll have the review back to you Friday afternoon. I'll send it to your email."

Genie said as she turned away from the office and towards the main room. She turned sharply and walked away. Her pace was a little faster than normal. Margaret called after Genie as she raced out of the room.

"Goodbye, Genesis, I'll see you next Monday."

Genie called behind her shoulder as she skipped down the stairwell, "Goodbye Ms. Margaret."

Genie could smell the brewing coffee from the top of the stairwell. She sped down the stairs and held the banister. When she reached the bottom, she let go of the banister and reached for the handle of the door that separated the upstairs office space and the quaint shop in the lower level. As she opened the door, she felt the warmth of the small shop. More than anything, Genie wanted to stay in the warm shop and sit in the seat that her and Tyler had shared only a few nights ago. Genie knew that she couldn't stay though. Since her sister had come home on Saturday afternoon, Genie had only eaten two meals with her. She had been avoiding any unnecessary contact with Trinity. Now, she had to spend the evening with her family. Noah and Poppy didn't bother her, it was her mother and sister that drove her up a wall. When together, they formed this evil force that set out to make Genie look bad. No matter what she did, she couldn't avoid the cruel intent of the women in her family. Her father would have made things easier but he wasn't there to help. Genie pushed open the door of the coffee shop and resisted the cold air as it surrounded her. She ran to her car and was close to being inside the safety of her car when the rain began to fall. Rain in March was the worst form of precipitation there was. It was cold and chilled the poor souls that it soaked to their bones. Genie rushed into her car and closed the door quickly. She looked at herself in the rearview mirror. Her cheeks had become permanently red over the winter season and she never seemed to look as relaxed as she did in the summer months. If she kept up this tense look by the time she was thirty she'd have wrinkles and worry lines that would last a lifetime. She turned on her car and gripped the steering wheel. She drove home in around six minutes, which was fairly quick for her. When she pulled up to her home, it glowed with lively activity. Inside, she could see Noah running around, most likely bothering his mother. Trinity was coming down the stairwell. It was a wonder what you could see from looking inside the front window. Genie proceeded to open and close the gate and enter her house as quietly as possible. She was halfway up the stairs when Trinity's piercing voice. stopped her.

"Genie, where have you been?"

Genie stopped, closed her eyes and turned.

She skipped down the steps and was surprised to see Trinity waiting for her at the bottom. Trinity was wearing light denim jeans, a white dress shirt, and a pastel yellow cardigan. Genie thought she looked like school bus. The thought of Trinity pulling up alongside a group of children made her laugh inside. They'd scream and say she was the meanest bus around. Genie could barely contain a smile. These were the crazy things that went on in her head. Genie stared into Trinity's snakelike eyes.

"I picked up my topic from the paper."

Trinity made an 'o' with her mouth and put one hand on the banister. Genie was three steps up from the bottom of the staircase where Trinity had trapped her in.

"That's lovely, what is your topic this week?"

Genie groaned on the inside, she really didn't want to have a conversation with her sister right now.

"I have to go to this Art Exhibition tomorrow. So I won't be home for dinner tomorrow."

Trinity looked surprised and replied, "Well, that sounds interesting. Why don't I come with you? It would be fun. Like a mini road trip, just us sisters."

The way that Trinity had put it was meant to make it seem more appealing for her to come but she had just made it seem more like a prison sentence than an enjoyable evening.

"That's okay, really, I'll be fine," Genie said turning away from her sister and taking a few steps up the stairs.

"I'll tell mom not to expect us for dinner tomorrow," Trinity said turning towards the kitchen.

Genie couldn't believe what a witch her sister was. Anger welled up inside of her as her steps on the stairs turned more into stomps. She burst into her room and plopped down on her bed. She pulled her phone out of her pocket. She flew through her contacts down to T. After two rings, Tyler picked up.

"Hey."

Genie was quick to answer.

"She's a monster."

Tyler sighed before continuing, "I know that you don't get along with your sister but think about it this way, she'll be gone on Sunday. Trinity no more."

Genie huffed and got up from her bed.

"I have to go to this art show tomorrow and she's coming with me."

A pot or pan clattered to the floor downstairs.

"I am relatively concerned that I might murder her," Genie said looking out her window.

Tyler laughed, "Well, try to stay away from tempting sharp objects. Why are you going to the art show anyway?"

Genie watched as a mini-van pulled into the driveway across the street.

"The paper and I really don't want to go."

Tyler replied, "Go, enjoy yourself. It'll be fine. There'll be free food and you will learn a little something I'm sure."

Tyler was right. It couldn't be all that bad. People did this for a living. There had to be some excitement involved.

"Thanks Ty, are we still on for Friday? I don't think Addie will be joining us."

"If neither of us has plans, then I'll pick up a movie," Tyler replied as Genie sat back down on her bed.

"OK, I gotta go. Bye"

"Bye."

With that, Genie ended the call and threw her phone back onto her bed.

She sat and looked around her room. Her walls were a light blue and her comforter was polka dotted brown and blue. There were posters of her favorite athletes and celebrities on the wall. On the mirror that sat on her dresser were pictures and football tickets that she had taped around the edges. Her room was definitely a reflection of all that she had been a part of in the last couple years. She thought about the art show and came to the conclusion that she wouldn't let anything make her unhappy, not a boring art show and not her evil sister.

Chapter 8

Genie sat in the passenger seat of her sister's car. Trinity had just finished babbling on about how wonderful this guy she had met was. Apparently, his name was Ben and he was a junior at Maryland. He and Trinity had a psychology class together and he had helped her study for one of the big tests before the winter break. They had gone out to dinner once or twice but "nothing big" as Trinity had said. She also said that he had called her twice since she had been home but she had ignored his call in an attempt to play "hard to get." Trinity playing hard to get was like the Joker dressing up as Batman for Halloween. It just didn't work.

During the entire car ride, Genie had said about ten words, and she had only said that many because she didn't want to get lectured about being a bad listener or being rude. Genie glanced down at the paper that she had resting on her lap. The map had said it would take them 26 minutes to get to the Art Center and 33 minutes had already passed and they still weren't there.

"Hey Trinity, do you know where you're going?"

Trinity groaned and looked over at Genie, "Yes, I had several piano concerts there. Don't you remember?"

Unfortunately, Genie did. Trinity used to be passionate about playing the piano and twice a year, the whole family was forced to go to the Art Center to sit for three hours and listen to other people's children struggle through musical pieces before Trinity preformed her two classical pieces. Of course, Trinity would blow the crowd away with her prodigy level talent. It was all sickening memories.

Now, it was ten minutes before Genie was told to be there and they still hadn't arrived. Trinity turned onto a street that led into a wooded neighborhood.

"Where are you going?" Genie heard herself ask.

Trinity rolled her eyes and responded shortly, "I know where I am going, thank you very much."

Genie pressed her forehead against the window and watched as the small 70's style houses passed. Trinity stopped at a stop sign and turned onto a different street. Then, in the distance, Genie could see the Art Center. Located in a wooded neighborhood, the Art Center was an old white barn that looked run down from the outside.

As Trinity parked, Genie grabbed her pocket notebook and unbuckled her seat belt. When Trinity took the key out of the engine, Genie jumped out of the car. Her black heels hit the ground with a clack. She rushed ahead so that she wouldn't be anywhere near her sister until it was time to leave.

Genie had on a short, black skirt and a pink pin stripe dress shirt. Her hair was partly pulled back giving her a very professional look. As she opened the door, the warmth of the center heated her pink cheeks. She walked in and gave the people sitting at the table in front her name. She held her notebook and pen and began to make her way around the show. There were about 50 people wandering around the beautiful art center. Many beautiful paintings were hung on the white walls. Genie made her way to one of the paintings on the far wall. It was unusual and she wasn't quite sure that she understood it. On a white canvas were thick black lines that stretched from one corner to the next. In between the four triangles formed by the lines were small thin red lines that looked very chaotic and unorganized. There were also flecks of purple here and there. What stood out from everything else in the piece was the large painting of a human eye in the center of the canvas. Genie stood staring at the canvas for a few minutes.

Then she heard a deep voice questioning "Do you get it?"

Genie looked over and saw a guy her age standing next to her, staring at the same piece she was. The guy had dirty blonde hair and he was wearing a casual black vest, unbuttoned, a white T-shirt that hugged his biceps and he had his hands in the pockets of his dark jeans. Genie was without an answer.

She finally spoke, "No, I don't actually. What about you?"

The guy turned towards her. Genie saw that he had dark green eyes. He took a step towards her and replied,

"Not really. Do you know anything about art?"

Genie shook her head no.

"Name's Carson, what about you?"

Genie turned towards him and got a really good look at him for the first time.

"Genie. Can you tell me anything about this piece? I have to write an article for my town's newspaper and I have no idea what to say about this.

Is this even art? I always thought art was beautiful paintings that depicted landscapes or something. Who's even the artist?"

Genie surprised herself with all the questions that she had just said out loud.

Carson turned to her again, "Ouch. It is called abstract art, Genie, and it happens to symbolize something."

Genie looked at him questioningly, "And what might it symbolize Mr. Carson?"

He laughed a little and replied,

"Well the black lines symbolize the confines of society and the prejudice ways of the American people. The red symbolizes all those who wish to revolt but cannot find courage and the purple flecks symbolize those who have the courage and choose not to stand up."

Genie was stunned, she jotted down a few notes.

"Well, since its obvious that you've talked to the artist, what did they tell you about the eye?"

"Well, he told me that the eye symbolized that when you try, it is easy to see through the tough exteriors that some people may show. That's what he told me anyway."

Genie nodded and looked around the room.

"Where is this exquisite artist? I kinda wanna meet him. What did you say his name was?"

Genie looked over at Carson just as he extended his hand.

"Carson Knight. Yeah, I kind of lied. I know what the painting's about. I'm the artist. See, you got to meet him."

Genie shook his hand surprised.

"I am so sorry, this is art, I just . . ."

"Don't worry about it," he said cutting her off, "I get that a lot. You don't seem to know a whole lot about art."

Genie laughed and replied, "no, you're right. I don't. I'm just here to write an article for my town's newspaper."

Carson began to walk towards her, "And where do you live?"

Genie smiled and answered, "Deal Island. It's a small town," but before she could finish, Carson cut her off,

"I know where it is. I just moved there. I don't know where you go to school but I'm a junior at the Blakeridge Academy, do you know,"

This time it was her turn to interrupt him.

"I'm a junior there too."

Carson looked shocked.

"Well, maybe you could show me around town sometime."

Genie could feel heat rising to her cheeks, "Maybe. I'd have to check my schedule," she said.

"Well, alright then. I'll see you at school tomorrow, ugh, Genie."

Genie nodded.

When Carson smiled and turned away, Genie felt herself blushing. She had just met a really cute guy. Maybe he was into her. She smiled and walked to another piece that was hanging from the ceiling. Genie studied it. She took a few notes and walked to the next piece. She was ready to leave. She walked around the large room for a few minutes and as she was sitting on a bench staring at a painting of a mother and child she caught a glimpse of Carson talking to a group of adults in suits and cocktail dresses. He looked over her way and smiled. She felt her insides swell and she quickly looked down at her shoes. Trinity was passing her to go see a sculpture when Genie stood and stepped in front of her.

"I'm ready to go."

Genie confronted he sister. They stood uncomfortably close, their noses two inches apart.

"Good to know," Trinity said stepping to the side of Genie.

"No, Trinity, please. Can we leave? I have all the notes that I need and I would really like to go. I have homework."

Trinity sighed and looked Genie in the eyes.

"Fine, let's go. I'm not happy though. I was enjoying myself."

Genie didn't care if Trinity was happy. It, sickly, made her happy that her sister was unhappy.

Trinity led the way to the exit and as they passed two elderly women, Trinity waved saying,

"Good evening, Susan, Trish.."

The two women waved goodbye each saying, "Goodbye Trinity."

If it were anyone else in the world that had made friends with two retired women, Genie would have been surprised. Trinity unlocked the car and Genie climbed in. As her sister started the engine, she noticed the time on the clock. They had only been in the show for half an hour.

When they had been driving for 10 minutes, Trinity looked over and asked, "So who was that guy that was talking to you?"

Genie tried not to blush at the thought of her and Carson's interaction.

"He's new at Blakeridge. His name is Carson. He asked me to show him around."

Trinity nodded then returned her eyes to the road.

"He looked pretty cute. I think I saw him in Mrs. Sims office on Monday morning."

Trinity was obviously trying to make conversation with her and Genie felt bad about ignoring her.

"Oh that's cool."

Trinity shrugged, "Maybe he's a trouble maker. You know since I saw him in the office and all," she offered.

Genie rolled her eyes. It was amazing that her sister had gotten straight A's whenever she had no common sense.

"No, his first day was Monday. That's why he was there. Plus, he was one of the artists at the show, I highly doubt he'd be getting into any serious trouble."

"Oh," Trinity responded, "well, I didn't see any of his work."

Genie looked over at her sister, "He had an abstract piece. His symbolism was quite deep."

Trinity nodded and replied, "Since when do you know anything about symbolism? Sounds like a good guy though. Maybe he could teach you something."

Chapter 9

Genie grabbed a few books from her locker and stuffed them into her bag. It was Friday and she couldn't be happier. It was her last class before lunch and at lunch; she would see Carson and maybe flirt a little more. She had already thought of what she'd say during history while Mrs. Jenkins babbled on about the Alamo. A Mexican battle was the last thing that crossed Genie's mind as she thought about Carson's sense of humor.

Genie went into study hall, happy to have some free time. The bell rang and the other students rushed into classrooms. Because it was a study hall, it didn't matter what time she got to the room as long as she got there at some point. Genie checked her makeup in the mirror and shut the door to her locker. She lifted her bag from the floor and slung it over her right shoulder. Her hair was pulled into a loose ponytail and it swayed as she walked down the hallway. She looked into the library's doorway as she passed. The gas fireplace looked calm and peaceful in the empty library. The library was the most beautiful part of the school. It was a two-story room that had ceiling rafters, a stone fireplace, and about a hundred wooden bookcases. Genie turned down a different hallway and stopped at a door. She opened the door and saw about half of the students that were usually in her study hall. She walked to her seat next to Addie and behind Tyler.

"Hey girlie," Addie said as Genie took her seat.

She looked up at Addie from her seat. Addie was going through an Algebraic expression.

"Hey, Addie," Genie said.

"What," Addie asked looking up from her notebook.

"I met a guy."

Tyler turned around and stared at Genie. There was a sign of disappointment in his eyes.

"Wait, you have a date?"

Genie shook her head and added, "Well, no, not yet. I mean I just met him last night."

She giggled but Tyler didn't loosen up. Genie's face suddenly saddened.

"Oh my gosh, Tyler, loosen up. It's no big deal."

Tyler shrugged and lied, "Yeah, okay. I think I'm gonna go see the game tonight."

Genie seemed surprised, "Oh really? Lindsey?"

Tyler nodded before continuing, "Yeah, she's been nagging me about not seeing her perform at the games. I'll call you tomorrow and tell you how things go."

Even though what Tyler said was believable, it didn't seem honest. There was a hint of pain and hurt in his voice.

"Oh good, I hope things go well with the blonde monster."

Genie said trying not to laugh. The three of them went back to working. Before she knew it, the bell was telling Genie that class was over. She stood and lifted her bag. As she lifted her bag, she turned to Addie and Tyler.

"Hey I'll see you guys at lunch. I'm gonna try to catch up with Carson."

"Ooh la la," Addie joked, nudging Genie.

"Alright, we'll see you later."

Addie said laughing and looping her arm through Tyler's. Genie watched them exit before attempting to leave.

As she entered the crowded hallway, she began to look for Carson. Students pushed past her and bumped into her making it hard to search for him. After a few minutes of walking around the hallway, she gave up and put her books in her locker. She grabbed her wallet and headed to the cafeteria. The cafeteria looked like a formal dining hall with small circular tables spread throughout the room. It had a college style cafeteria with the elegance of a formal dining room.

Genie looked around, searching for Tyler and Addie when she felt a tap on her shoulder. She whizzed around and found herself face to face with Carson.

"Hey, fancy meeting you here" he said.

Genie was surprised that he'd looked for her.

"Oh sure, um," she said reaching into her skirt pocket, pretending to look for something. Why was she being such a klutz?

He said watching her, "Are you going to the game tonight?"

"Uh, yeah, of course. Why?"

He looked down at his shoes.

"I don't know, maybe I'll see you there."

Genie watched as he turned and walked away. She turned and saw that

Addie was staring at her. Addie cocked her head and gave two thumbs up. Genie couldn't help but laugh. It was too good of a day.

Genie watched as the players ran out onto the court. The crowd roared and a few girls behind her screamed the names, "Nick! Cameron! Justin!" Three guys with sweat bands around their head turned and waved. Genie groaned. She didn't really want to be there but Carson said he'd be here so it was worth the pain of listening to those annoying girls behind her. Genie watched as the cheerleaders did a high kick and the crowd went wild. Lindsey was leading a few other cheerleaders in cartwheels across the gym floor. Their skirts went flying and the crowd cheered and clapped. Lindsey stood up, did another high kick and clapped. Her white teeth looked like pearls from where Genie sat. Lindsey winked and some people lower in the bleachers whistled. Is this what high school was all about? Had Genie missed a memo?

She exhaled sharply and waited for the game to start. Where was Addie when you needed her? Addie would have been making fun of those girls.

Now Genie sat alone, waiting for a guy she didn't even know that well. A small man in a black and white striped shirt walked to the middle of the court and the players lined up and faced each other. How much more boring could this get?

"Did you want salted or unsalted? I couldn't remember."

Tyler was making his way from the isle to where she was sitting. He was holding a small cardboard box and inside was a pretzel, a hotdog, and two drinks. He tried to get around the people who were already sitting on the row of the bleacher.

"Uh, either is fine."

He handed her the pretzel and she eyed it. Unsalted. He plopped down on the plastic bleacher.

"Crappy food has gotten expensive lately."

He squinted at the court. He had on a flannel shirt and jeans. His shirt was unbuttoned and he had on a cotton T-shirt underneath. He jerked his head and his hair was pushed away from his eyes.

"You missed it," Genie said taking a bite out of her pretzel, "Lindsey's ass made its public debut."

Tyler chuckled and put the box on his lap.

"Oh, darn."

He said taking a bite out of his hotdog. He was still staring at the field. By now the game had started and people were cheering.

"Mustang's own Cameron Barnet with a beautiful shot!"

The crowd cheered and Tyler looked at Genie.

"Is he really that good?"

Tyler was pathetic when it came to sports. He had played soccer until fourth grade and then they started separating who was good and who wasn't and he quit. His parents were into golf and tennis but no one had ever taught him a lick about basketball, football, or baseball.

"I'm pretty sure it means he's good if they just announced his name," Genie said.

"Oh," Tyler replied, "I guess I'll just go by the crowd. If they cheer, so do I."

"Sounds like a good plan."

Tyler and Genie sat and watched the game and soon the sky turned to black outside the gym windows. The whistle blew and the majority of the people on the bleachers stood up.

"Must be half time," she said standing.

"Oh," Tyler said taking a sip of his soda.

"I'm gonna take a walk. I'll be back before the game starts up again." Genie turned.

"Oh, yeah," he said grabbing some trash. "I better go see Lindsey and all. I'll catch you later."

He walked in the other direction. Genie felt kinda bad. He seemed so lost at the game, so out of place. She walked down the metal steps and stepped onto the court. The gym was kind of cold and giving her goose bumps. The majority of the students were walking around and talking. Most had food and some were making out behind corners.

Genie didn't see anyone she could talk to but there had to be someone from one of her classes that she knew. Molly Peterson was nice. She was standing with a few other girls. All four of them were wearing jeans and polos. Their hair was down with a clip pulling the front part of it back. They all looked exactly the same. Molly waved to Genie. She smiled and waved back. Genie started toward the group of girls when she felt a tap on her shoulder. She turned and was face to face with a gorgeous guy in a graphic T-shirt. Carson smiled.

"Hey," he said putting his hands in his pockets.

Genie's throat went dry.

"Oh, hi," she managed.

"So what do you think of the game?"

Genie hadn't really been paying attention. Even if she had, she had no idea what was good and bad.

"Uh, um, good I guess."

"Really," he said, "cause we're down by 18 points."

Her alarm clock said it was 8:30 and she knew that breakfast
[...] he table right now. She skipped down the stairs and the smell
[...] ed her. She held the banister and whirled around to face the
[...] nderson kitchen was painted yellow and had white cabinets
[...] lge. The white tile made the kitchen look clean and fresh.
[...] table sat in the corner of the kitchen.
[...] novel in her hands as she sat in the corner chair. Noah
[...] knees, with a piece of bacon hanging from his mouth.
[...] te little kid. He had light blonde hair that was neatly
[...] bout 4'10 and 70 pounds He had bright blue eyes and
[...] cheeks. Genie had never been all that close with Noah
[...] t more than Trinity. She liked the neighbor's kids more

[...] over a frying pan on the stove when Genie walked

[...] re is bacon and eggs on the table. Help yourself."
[...] little cold to Genie. Ellen and Trinity had always
[...] med as though there wasn't enough love for Trinity
[...] had favored her first. Ellen was a woman in her
[...] She was a small woman who had a blonde bob.
[...] nd pale skin. She seemed like an average mom

[...] had been very passionate about tennis. She
[...] husband at the middle school's tennis courts.
[...] ours, critiquing each other and enjoying the
[...] ird Sunday of every month, Ellen and Victor
[...] les to the local country club. They'd t[...]
[...] spouses for a f[...]

Genie could feel the heat rise to her cheeks. Oops.

"I take it you don't know much about basketball?"

He smiled. Okay so at least he knew why.

"Yeah, I really don't watch it often," she said smiling.

He chuckled and his eyes met hers.

"Uh, I don't know about you but I really don't wanna be here," he said.

Had he just read her mind?

"Yeah, me neither. I'm not really a big fan."

He laughed and took his right hand out of his pocket.

"I've got a car."

"Well, good for you. So do I," Genie said cutting him off.

He laughed at her snappy comment.

"Well, you guys got an ice cream place in this town?"

Genie smiled.

"Yeah, we do."

"How about you show me where that is and I'll reward you for your services."

She blushed. He was charming.

"How about we take my car?" She suggested.

"Alright. You drive."

She took a step towards the parking lot and he followed.

"I don't think we'll have to worry about this ice cream melting any time soon. It's freezing out here," Carson said licking a drop of chocolate ice cream off of his hand.

He smiled at Genie. She laughed.

"Yeah, it's a little chilly."

The drive over to the ice cream shop had been great. They had made fun of how ridiculous the basketball team was. They sucked. They always had. Carson was more into art than sports. He used to play hockey, he said but it got too expensive because of how coveted ice time was. Genie looked at him as he licked his scoop of chocolate. He noticed her looking and laughed.

"Not the most graceful way to eat, huh?"

She laughed and took a bite of her vanilla with rainbow sprinkles. She was a little kid at heart when it came to sprinkles. Carson had paid and they were both enjoying their dessert. He looked over at her.

"So, what do you like to do?"

"Um, I write . . . a lot. Ha-ha. I go to church a lot. I don't know if that counts as what I like to do but my family does go to church a lot. My mom's really into it. I, uh, like to watch movies. I'm into the oldies. I don't play any sports currently."

article to [...]
finishing tou[...]
"That's alr[...]
"Okay, than[...]
Arnold seemed [...]
her. Maybe he got so[...]
whatever was wrong wit[...]
She clicked send and [...]
sent" appeared on her lapt[...]
[...]rds "your message has been
[...]e rose from her bed and walked out

"H[...]orted [...]
[...]or emotion, or

59

Carson looked surprised.

"Oh, wait, so you mean you aren't one of the cheerleaders? Shoot, I thought it was just your day off," he said sarcastically.

She laughed and their eyes met.

"Well," he said pushing himself away from her. "I don't know if I'm interested in a girl who can't do a backflip. I'm sorry."

"Oh I'm sorry. I can give it a shot," she said standing up.

She handed him the cone and leaned back a little.

"Holy crap! You're not gonna actually do it, are you?"

She laughed and took back her cone.

"I can't even do a summersault. Do you actually think I'd flip for you?"

"I don't know. You never said you weren't crazy."

"Well, I am."

He laughed and looked her in the eye,

"Good."

Chapter

Genie sat on h
finished writing h
send it yesterda
send it. Right

Che
Ge

of her room.
would be on
of bacon sooth
kitchen. The A
and a white fri
A small, circula
Trinity held
was sitting on his
Noah was a c
cut. He was only a
freckles covered his
but she liked him a l
than she liked Trinity
in.
Ellen was standin

"Hello, Genesis, th
Ellen was always a
been very close and it see
and Genie both and Elle
late 40's that stood at 5'5
She had bright blue eyes a
but Genie knew differently.
Before Victor died, Elle
spent every Saturday with he
They played each other for h
time they spent together. The t
would go with a few other cou
opponents and play each other
the lockers and heading to brunc
love of tennis until she found a p
Genie loved to write and she
write once a week except for every
had only picked up her racket long
sad to think that her mother's passi
husband. Now, Ellen was speaking w
"Morning, Noah."
Noah looked at Genie and smiled.
"Hey, Tyler's gonna be here in a l
box derby thing." Genie nodded as sh
was always hereto help Noah with some
do already, Tyler made something for the
already showered and had her hair pulled

absolutely nothing exciting about her family this morning so she decided to go back to her room and see if there was anything more exciting there. Genie was just at the top of the staircase when her phone began to ring. She rushed in and pressed the phone to her ear without looking to see who it was. A deep voice rang through the earpiece.

"Good Morning, sunshine."

Carson. Genie was happy to hear from him.

"Ha ha, good morning. I'm glad you called."

"Oh? And why is that?"

Genie smiled coyly even though she knew he couldn't see her.

"I wanted to let you know that you should pick up the paper tomorrow. I put you in the paper."

"I'm flattered. Did you tell all of Deal Island what a stud I was and what great ice cream we had?"

Genie laughed.

"No. I'll be sure to put it in next week's article. It was about your piece at the art show."

Carson chuckled and said, "I didn't think it was all that good."

"I thought it was intriguing."

"Liar," he said, "you didn't even think it was art at first."

"I'm still learning," she laughed.

"Hey, you wanna go and do something today?"

"Sure," Genie answered. "

All right, cool, I'll pick you up at 12. Bundle up."

Genie giggled, "Okay bye."

"Bye."

She had another date with Carson and she'd only known him for three days. Genie smiled thinking of what they could possibly be doing later. Bundle up. Did that mean that they would be outside because it was very cold in March? Genie was opening the doors to her closet when the doorbell rang.

Genie caught a glimpse of herself in the mirror. She hadn't showered yet and her hair was pulled into a messy bun. Her black yoga pants sat on her hips loosely. She wore a blue tank top and her green toenails looked extremely bright against her pale feet. She turned out of her room and walked to the top of the staircase. When she looked down, Noah was hugging Tyler's legs. Tyler looked like he hadn't gotten any sleep the night before. Tyler waved and Genie smiled. Tyler looked down at Noah and Genie could barely make out what he was saying.

"I'll be right back."

Tyler passed Noah and climbed the staircase. Genie waited until he had reached the top before she turned to go back to her room.

"Hey, I didn't know you were coming over this early."

Tyler smiled, "Yeah. I'm here to help Noah but I wanted to talk to you about something."

"Oh," Genie said sitting on her bed.

Tyler followed and sat next to her.

"I broke up with Lindsey."

Genie gasped.

"Wait?" "What?" "Why?"

Tyler exhaled and laid back. He was lying on his back staring at the ceiling.

"Well, I showed up at the court yesterday and I watched her practice before the game started up again. I could've sworn that she saw me. Anyway, the game started and I watched. She did her cheer thing well, I guess. Well, as you know, many of the players have girlfriends on the team and after the game; the players went after their chicks. I started walking down the bleachers to get her when Trevor Harris, you know who that is, well he went up to her and kissed her. Right then and there. That's when I realized that it didn't bother me all that much. I really don't have feelings for her. So I sent her a text that said that I thought we should see other people. Since I knew she had already gotten started on that."

Tyler looked tired but not upset.

"Oh, Ty," Genie said reaching her arms out.

Tyler fell into them. His muscles were loose and he seemed unusually cold. Tyler sat back up.

"Wait, how was your night?"

Genie looked at him and saw the way he stared at her with curiosity. Genie smiled.

"It was really good actually. We had ice cream and stuff. We're going out today. He's picking me up at noon. He said bundle up. What do you think we'll do?"

Tyler chuckled which made Genie immediately feel self-conscious.

"I don't know but I'm sure he'll show you a good time."

Genie squinted and raised an eyebrow. Tyler seemed unusually trusting and calm. Tyler rose from the bed and looked down at her. His brown eyes sparkled and she knew that any jealousy or suspicion that he may have had was dismissed. He walked out of the room and hopped down the stairs. Genie stared in the mirror and noticed that she didn't look all the bad after all.

Chapter 11

Carson's car was small and beaten up and old. Genie liked the way it was small and how warm it was. Genie watched as Carson drove away from her house and onto the neighborhood's main road.

"So, it seems like you have a lovely home," Carson said looking over to Genie.

She smiled and returned his comment with, "You didn't get to see much. It is really great. I live with my mom and grandpa."

Carson nodded and held one hand on the wheel.

"Any siblings?"

He asked staring at the road.

"Unfortunately . . . I have a great little brother, Noah. He's 10. Then there's my sister, Trinity. She's the unfortunate part. She's eighteen and in college at Maryland."

Carson looked over in her direction.

"I noticed that your brother and sister have religious names but you don't."

Genie sighed but smiled.

"Being honest, my full name is Genesis but I go by Genie. So we all have religious names." Carson laughed softly and asked, "What's with that? I mean, I've heard Mary, Elizabeth, John, Joseph, hell, I've heard Jesus but I don't think I've heard Genesis and Trinity."

Carson watched as Genie laughed.

"Yeah, my parents are unique."

Carson nodded and returned his gaze to the road.

"I don't have many siblings. I had a brother, Landon, but when my parents divorced, he went with my dad. I can see why, I mean he was 11 and he wanted a male figure. I chose my mom because I knew she needed me."

"Wow, that's really . . . responsible and deep. It must have been hard on you and your brother."

Carson's eyes met Genie's and she could tell what pain the whole experience had brought him.

"Yeah but I've moved on. It was a couple of years ago now."

Genie nodded. She took note of how amazingly gorgeous he was. He was about 6'2 and he had huge muscles. He had a crew cut, which fit him well. He looked like he'd just finished basic training for the army. He didn't look tough though, more gentle. She also noticed that his eyes weren't hazel like they seemed in the dark but a darker green. He had discreet dimples and he was just perfect. Why had he chosen her? She thought maybe that he would rather go out with someone really pretty like Lindsey. Well, Lindsey wasn't super pretty but she had her days. Genie had an elf face. What was cute about that? Genie looked out the window when her thoughts were interrupted by his voice.

"So I found this restaurant called Pizza Shack. I don't know if you've heard of it."

Genie laughed out loud. He was undoubtedly funny.

"I don't know, it seems risky," she said giggling.

He laughed then returned his eyes to the road. He pulled into the parking lot of the Pizza Shack. He took the keys out of the ignition and opened the door. Unlike in Tyler's truck, Genie had no problem getting out of Carson's car. It was fairly low to the ground. She followed him and entered into the rundown building as he held the door open for her. The pizza place smelled great and it reminded her of Noah because pizza was his favorite food and his obsession. Carson walked to the counter before turning to Genie.

"Hey, I'm going to order some pizza, is cheese okay?"

Genie nodded and answered, "I'm gonna be in the bathroom."

Carson nodded and gave her another amazingly white smile. Genie kept her head down as she walked across the small restaurant to the door with the animated woman on it. She pushed open the door and stood in front of one of the three mirrors. She stared at her reflection. Her makeup was perfect and her hair was straightened and pulled back with a sparkly clip. She examined her outfit. Her black and white checkered shirt hung over her black skinny jeans, which were tucked into her black boots. She looked good. She turned to leave the bathroom. She pulled the door open and looked for Carson. When she found him, he was sitting at a table by himself in the corner, with his hands intertwined over the box of pizza. She smiled and walked over to the table.

"Well, as lovely as this place is, I thought that maybe we'd take this someplace else."

As Carson said this, Genie's thoughts immediately went negative. She was a little worried about being alone with him. Was he going to try and make a move? She really didn't want to go there yet.

As he stood from the table and grabbed the box, he leaned in and whispered in her ear, "I swear, I'm not gonna try to seduce you. I swear."

It was in a joking way but it meant the world to her to hear that.

As he leaned away she caught his eyes and they flickered with honesty. She followed him out of the restaurant and back to his old car. The pizza's smell drifted all over the car and Genie could hear her stomach growl.

"Where are we going?"

She asked looking at him.

Carson turned his head without letting his eyes leave the road, "I know I've only been here for a couple weeks but I've already found a favorite place and I want to take you there."

Genie couldn't help but feel special. As Carson drove, they talked about simple things. Genie had told him about Tyler and Addie. When she had mentioned Tyler, Carson didn't seem to be jealous or suspicious at all. Genie wasn't sure if he should have been but it seemed appropriate if he questioned her and Tyler's relationship. When they stopped at a stoplight, Carson looked over at her.

"You know, you are much prettier here than under those God awful lights at the Art Center."

Genie blushed and tried to think of a clever comment, "Well you look much better now than standing in front of those awful old people."

Carson laughed out loud and chuckled all the way up until he parked the car.

"Where are we?"

Genie opened the door and got out to look around. Even though it was a small town, Genie hadn't been to some of the older and abandoned places. Carson reached in and grabbed the pizzas from the backseat.

"Here, follow me."

Genie followed Carson as he slowly walked down a small but steep hill. Below the hill were the waters of the bay. Genie's heartbeat sped up. She was worried about slipping and falling into the water. Carson must have sensed her fear because he reached his arm back and took hold of her skinny arm. He guided her down to a wooden dock. He walked across the pier and when he got to the end, he sat down. Genie was a few feet behind him and in her mind she questioned why he chose this spot. Of all the places on Deal Island, the old pier behind the bait shop would not have been where she would have taken a date. The hill that had brought them to the pier looked eerie. Genie went and sat next to him on the edge of the pier. They both sat crisscross near the edge. Genie stared at Carson as he watched the waves toss and turn.

"I know that this place may not seem like much to you, but ever since I moved here, it's been the only place that I could be alone and I like it."

Genie stared at him and her heart melted at the innocence and honesty he shared with her.

"Yeah, I love the water. I've always thought it was the most beautiful and pure part of this town," Genie explained as she reached for a slice of pizza. Carson leaned back on his palms.

"It seems so harmless even though you and I both know water can do some pretty powerful shit."

Genie laughed at his comment and he looked at her smiling. His dimples were calming her nerves.

"Oh, wait, I'm sorry do you cuss? I didn't mean to . . . ," he backtracked.

"Its fine," she assured him, "I'm not perfect."

"Could've fooled me."

Genie couldn't help but blush. He knew exactly what to say.

"So where did you live before you moved here?" Genie asked, chewing a mouth full of cheese.

Carson returned his gaze to the water.

"I lived in D.C. My mom thought it was a little too rough. She said she wanted to see me get acquainted with a small town."

Genie giggled, "Deal Island small enough for you?"

Carson chuckled and moved closer to Genie. Part of her wanted him to kiss her and another part wanted him to ask her to marry him. He was perfect.

He slipped his arm around her and she felt his solid bicep against her shoulder. He was definitely strong and trying not to hurt her. The wind blew and with it brought the scent of his cologne. Genie smiled and leaned in close to him.

"It's kinda weird because we only met a few days ago but I feel like I know you better than I know some of my friends back home."

Genie almost died when he said this. He was a real charmer.

"Yeah, I mean, I feel like we could be kinda . . . I don't know . . . close friends."

Genie melted with every word. He looked at her and their eyes caught. He tilted his head and leaned in. Genie wanted to but she stopped him.

"We only met on Thursday."

Carson nodded and backed away.

"I understand. I was moving a little fast. This is only our first official date. Apparently, I didn't get the memo about ice cream runs not counting as dates."

Genie laughed then looked at him questioningly, "Why did you choose me?"

"What do you mean," he asked.

"Well, there are a lot of really pretty girls at Blakeridge and any of them would be lucky to go out with you. Why'd you ask me out?"

Carson looked at the waves.

"Because you were different. You seem to know who you are and don't need the head cheerleader to tell you what to say. You are just a different kind of beautiful. Plus, you had no problem telling me that my art sucked."

Genie laughed.

"Well, you were right about the head cheerleader thing. I've never been a fan of girls in short skirts."

"I am," Carson said laughing.

Genie nudged him playfully. Okay, so he wasn't superhuman. He was still a 16-year-old guy. Genie's phone beeped and she pulled it out of her jean pocket. Carson reached for another piece of pizza as Genie glanced at her phone. Addie had sent her a text saying:

R u baq yet???? Call me wen u get home. Is he super hot?
What about sweet? AHH tell me everything! L8r luv

Carson laughed.

"What are you gonna tell her? Am I super hot?"

Genie was kind of mad that he had read her text but quickly snapped back, "Maybe . . . maybe not."

Carson looked offended.

"Really? Well, then, whenever I call Addie, I'll tell her that you didn't look that hot either."

Genie laughed. He had a great sense of humor. They both laughed and stared at the water. Carson looked at her.

"I should probably get you home."

Genie nodded and began to stand. Carson grabbed the box of pizza and when they got to the hill, he had his hand on her back the entire climb up. She liked the way he kept her safe. He threw the box out when they got to the top of the hill. As she got into his car, she stared out at the water and knew that the water would always be her favorite part of the town.

"The body of Christ."

"Amen."

Genie watched as each person walked up for Communion. She kneeled in the pew and bowed her head. She was in Church and the only thing she could think about was Carson. It was wrong and unholy. There was no commandment that said "thou shalt not think of hot guys while thou is in church-ith" but it seemed like it was wrong anyway.

A curl fell from its clip and swung into her vision as she stared at the person in the pew in front of hers shoes. White heels were very classy. She reached up and fixed her hair. Ellen looked over with one eye open and eyed Genie. She nudged her daughter.

"Can you try to pay attention?"

Genie's mouth dropped open. Noah leaned back from the other side of Ellen and stuck his tongue out. Genie's family was so annoying. They were bugging her because she was a little out of it. A line of people were passing where she sat. She watched as one by one, people received Communion. Finally, the priest sat down in his chair. Everyone shifted from kneeling to sitting in the pews. The priest stood and raised his hands over the assembly. They all made the sign of the cross.

"May you go in peace to love and serve the Lord," he said. The congregation replied, "Amen."

The piano player began and everyone stood. Ellen picked up her bag and pushed Genie out of the pew. What was with her family today? Her heels were bothering her and she couldn't wait to go home and take them off.

Sundays at the Anderson house were for relaxing. They rarely went out unless it was for brunch or to dinner. Poppy would usually sit and read the paper. Noah would play with the neighbor's kids or work on his projects. Ellen would read a novel out on the porch and Genie would do homework or write. They were like the perfect family except for dad.

Sundays were when Genie missed him the most. She used to read to him on Sundays after church and they'd make cookies together in the winter. Sundays just weren't the same. Whenever he died, the Church they went to, St. Bernadette's, was very supportive and kind. The priest would stop by every other day and talk with Ellen. He taught her how to pray and use faith as a crutch whenever times got tough. Ellen had never been the same. Genie remembered answering the door and women would be standing there with trays and platters of food sending their condolences. Everyone at the church seemed so friendly, caring, and compassionate. The Anderson family would be forever grateful.

The priest was standing outside of the Church doors as they exited as a family. He spread his arms out and Ellen walked right into them.

"It's good to see you again, Ellen."

He was an older man who had a wrinkled and aging face but youthful and vibrant eyes. He didn't seem old at all. The way he carried himself, you'd think he was in his 30's.

"Thank you, Father Duggan. I can't wait until the Easter season begins. I'm looking forward to your interesting Homily. It's also great to see people come together for the holiday."

Easter and Christmas were the two days that every Christian in town managed to make it to Church. Father Duggan smiled and shook Noah's hand.

Noah smiled, "Hi, Father."

"Hello, Noah. I heard you are participating in the pine box derby with the Boy Scouts. I'll be anxious to see who wins."

Noah's smile stretched from ear to ear.

"Well, I can tell you now, it's gonna be me!"

Poppy, Ellen, Father, and Genie laughed. Noah was really excited for the race. An older couple stepped up to Father Duggan, so the Andersons turned away.

"I didn't see the Moore's. Is someone sick?" Ellen asked Genie.

Addie and Tyler went to St. Bernadette's too. They were kind of active in the church but not as much as the Anderson family.

"Oh, not that I know of. Maybe they just didn't want to come today."

"Oh," Ellen said looking at her purse. "Maybe."

Genie walked along the stone path that led through the church's garden and to the parking lot.

"I need to go pick up some eggs and chips. Do you all mind?"

Everyone stared at Ellen as they climbed into the car.

"I guess not," Poppy said closing the passenger seat door.

"All right then. I'll be quick."

They drove to the grocery store and Ellen parked close to the building. Noah was in khaki pants and a red polo. He looked like a little man. Genie stared down at her ensemble. She was wearing unflattering black dress pants, a gray sweater, and a black blouse. Her hair was greasy because she hadn't showered since yesterday morning. She looked like a wreck. She didn't care much because she was going to the grocery store, not the Oscars. Ellen speed walked through the isles and grabbed a carton of eggs. Noah had already gone to the seasonal isle to look at the toys and videos for sale. Genie stood by the magazine stand. She was reading about the upcoming spring fashion shows when something caught the corner of her eye. She walked over to register three. An older man buying pizza for one, a gallon of ice cream, and pepper was checking out. Genie got in line behind him. She grabbed a bag of M&M's off the candy rack. The man took his change and when the cashier looked up and saw who was next, he smiled.

"Well, we seem to find each other a lot," Carson said.

Genie blushed.

"Yeah," she said, "I didn't know you worked here."

"Oh sure," he said teasingly leaning back on the small barrier.

"I'm serious. I'm here with my family. We just came from church."

"Oh so you weren't kidding about the whole religious thing."

Genie looked down and realized she was wearing a cross chain. Her family did look like a walking model of the perfect American church ad.

"Uh, yeah, we're kinda into it."

He laughed and looked at his feet.

"Yeah, well, you can see this place is just really busy, so I'm going to need to check you out here, miss," he said winking and taking the M&M's from her hand, sliding them across the scanner.

Beep.

"That'll be a dollar and six cents."

Genie reached into her purse and pulled out two singles.

"Your change is ninety-four cents."

His hand brushed hers as he gave her the coins. Her heart raced. Electric charged through her arm. Genie turned away smiling.

"Hey," he said, "are you doing anything later?"

She turned and stared into his greenish-hazel eyes.

"Not that I know of. I'd have to check with my family. I mean, we're busy as it comes."

Her family was approaching looking as lame as humanly possible. Were they trying to make her look bad? Noah was jumping around and begging Ellen for a candy bar.

"Well, I guess I'll pick you up at say two-ish. I don't wanna get you back too late. I mean it is a school night," he said in a sarcastic mother-ish tone.

She laughed and nodded. Ellen waved for Genie to come. Carson turned and watched as she went. Genie could feel her heart racing. Was it possible to have this rapid of a heart rate and not die?

"Not fair! Genie got candy!"

Noah was pointing at the M&Ms. Ellen looked disgusted and gave Genie the you-really-had-to-start-this look. Poppy smiled and tapped Noah on the back.

"She had to go see her boyfriend."

Genie could feel her eyes widen. They were still in the store!

"Oooohh," Noah said making a kiss face. "Is that him!?"

Noah said pointing at Carson who was still watching.

"Shut up! He's not my . . ."

Before she could finish, Ellen cut her off.

"Noah stop. Genie, we'll talk about this when we get home."

How could Ellen have turned this around to where it was Genie's fault? Noah was the one making a public disturbance. They finally exited the store but it was too late. She was mortified. The ride home was silent apart from Noah making kissing noises. Poppy thought the whole thing was laughable. Genie pressed her head against the window and tried her best not to explode and kill her brother. Ellen just stared emotionless at the road. Rain had begun to slowly fall. It splashed against the windshield and the wipers moved from one side of the glass to the other. Genie wanted to be out of the car and in her room, staring at the clock, waiting for two o'clock.

Chapter 12

"You ready to go?"

Carson was standing on Genie's porch, hands in pockets. Genie answered his question swiftly, "Yeah. Let me just let my mom know I'm leaving."

Genie was standing in the doorway, looking down at him. Carson was clad in jeans, and a black fleece. He had a T-shirt on but you could barely see it due to the fact that his jacket was zipped almost completely. Genie turned and looked straight into the kitchen where her mother was cooking lunch. From the aroma, Genie guessed grilled cheese.

"Mom, Carson's here. I'll be back soon. Bye."

"Goodbye, Genesis."

Genie turned and shut her front door behind her.

Carson looked over at her, "I just can't get over that whole Genesis thing."

Genie laughed and raised part of her lip.

"Is it really that bad?"

As they walked along the paved pathway that led to the driveway, she moved side by side with Carson.

He looked down to her, "Yeah, it's that bad."

Genie hit him playfully, "You're not supposed to say that."

There was a bit of whine in her voice.

Carson nudged her back, "You know I'm kidding."

"Maybe I do, maybe I'm offended."

"Aw, I'm sorry. I think your name is sexy. It really turns that little, bible reading, school boy part of me on."

"Shut up!"

The two of them came to his car. The old car was an awful beige that she hadn't noticed before. Carson jogged around to the passenger side. He opened the door and gestured towards the seat. He was impersonating a chauffeur and it only made Genie a little calmer. He was fun, not serious and he clearly wasn't going to try to make a move on her, not today at least. Genie slipped in and he shut the door before jogging around the front of the car to the driver's side. As he opened the door, a burst of cold air filled the small sedan. For the past couple weeks, the temperature had stayed below 55.

"Brrrr! It's pretty cold out there."

Genie said looking at him. He smiled and his dimples made an appearance. Genie's heart leapt and she again took notice as to just how good looking he was. He turned the key and the engine revved. He put his arm on her seat and turned to back out of her driveway. Tyler's red truck was parked a little beyond the mailbox.

"Something tells me the pick up isn't your sister's ride."

Genie chuckled, "No, that would be Tyler's. My sister's car is the oh-so-practical compact in the garage. Heaven forbid her baby withstand the elements."

Carson laughed and looked out the window.

"So what's with this Tyler guy? Is he a cousin or ex boyfriend? . . ."

Carson trailed off. Genie cleared her throat and looked in the direction of the glove box.

"He is . . . my friend. He's also Noah's best friend which is why he was there today."

"I had no idea Addie doubled as a Tyler on the weekends."

Genie couldn't help but let out a hearty laugh.

"No, I have two best friends. Ironic as it is, Addie and Tyler are twins."

Carson nodded before snagging a glimpse of Genie.

"Ah, I see. Were you and . . . ah . . . Tyler ever an item?"

He said item and accentuated the 't'. Genie had to think about his question. Were they ever an item? Tyler and Genie had kissed twice in the past eight days. Did that mean they had feelings for each other?

"No," Genie said.

"Alright," Carson said with one hand on the wheel, and the other arm around the back of her seat, "just checking my competition."

Genie willed herself not to blush.

"So where exactly are we going?"

She asked, trying to change the subject.

"You'll see."

"What is with you and surprises? Once and a while, I'm gonna want some real answers."

Carson looked her straight in the eyes.

"Once and while, you'll get some."

His voice deepened and his eyes seemed to tell a tale of mystery and charm. Genie couldn't wait to see where he was taking her. Carson pulled up to a large building. He parked and opened his door.

"What are we doing here?"

Genie asked feeling herself getting nervous and excited.

"Well, I thought I might show you something," Carson answered calmly.

"What is it?"

Genie barely got the words out before he grabbed her hand and pulled her behind him as he ran to the doors. His grip was tight and he pulled her a good 30 yards. Genie squealed and followed right after him.

"Close your eyes."

She had never liked closing her eyes. The last time she did that other than with Tyler was when she was ten and Trinity made her over to look like a clown. She obeyed and sealed her eyes. He led her inside and she felt the air warm.

"Hey, Rob. I'll be a little while. No big, right?"

Carson was talking to someone but Genie couldn't see whom.

"Yeah, no problem, Car. There isn't a practice till five."

Practice? She could hear a door open and the air smelled like chlorine and it was cold again. Were they at the indoor pool? The smell wasn't that strong though. She heard another door open and he stopped walking. He let go and stepped away.

"Open."

Genie's eyelids flipped open. They were in the middle of an ice rink. When he looked back at her, his expression was bright and he was biting his lower lip. Those dimples mocked her as she stood on the solid ice.

He grabbed and jerked her arm, "Ahhh!"

Genie was thrown across the ice. Her pink Converse slid on the ice and Genie extended her arms to try and balance herself. Carson let go and Genie slid four feet from him. She watched his smile get smaller as she slid away from him. He had some type of skateboarding shoe on and he was just as inadequately dressed as she was. Her hair blew around her face and she had just stopped sliding when her feet came out from under her. She hit the ice with a thump but she felt no pain as she watched Carson run on the ice. He slid quickly over to where she sat on the ice. They were alone on an ice rink in a place she'd never been before. Carson plopped down on the ice next to her.

"So?"

He raised his eyebrows looking at her.

"So what?"

He brought his knees up and rested his hands on his knee caps.

"So are you pissed or pleased?"

Genie got to her feet and looked down at him and winked.

"I'll let you know."

Just as she said that, she turned from him and ran on the ice. She was careful not to lose her balance as she ran away. She could hear him getting up. She tried to run away but he was too fast. Just as Genie looked up at the hockey banners hanging from the ceiling, Carson wrapped his hands around her. She squealed as he lifted her off of the ice. He brought her to the cold, hard ice gently. The cold air bit at her cheeks.

"What made you bring me here?"

He put his hands behind his head. He looked as though he was lounging on a beach in the Caribbean.

"Well, I told you I used to play hockey. Well, there are fewer teams around here so I looked into getting back into it. I've been drilling myself here for the last week."

"Oh," she said turning towards him. "So you actually know what your doing?"

He laughed, "Nope, I've never tried without skates before."

Just as they both lay on the ice laughing, music began. It wasn't cheesy love songs but the popular songs that filled every radio station.

"And I also have never been with someone like you so to answer your question, I have no idea what I'm doing."

Genie turned her head and looked at Carson. He turned his head and looked at her. His dark green eyes seemed to see right through all her pain and they touched her heart. She stood and tried to spin around but once again, she found herself being lifted off the ice. As she looked down at him, their eyes met. He smiled and Genie felt her feet touch the ice. He leaned in and closed his eyes. Genie did the same. When their lips met, she couldn't feel the cold. The ice that was clumped around her only made the moment feel more magical. The building seemed silent and uninhabited but at the same time, full of life. He held her neck and her arms were wrapped around his hips. They stood for minutes, holding each other, in the middle of the rink as the music played around them. Genie stared at him and even though her fingers were beginning to ache with the cold, she couldn't have thought of a more romantic moment. She looked down and saw his hands around her brown jacket. Her jeans were wet from the ice. Her hair, which she had curled, was already messed up but she didn't care. Carson grabbed her hand and led her slowly across the ice. They slid gracefully along the ice in silence. Carson looked over at her as they walked on the ice,

"You know you're even more beautiful with ice in your hair than you are in crappy art show lighting, or on an old dock."

Genie didn't laugh this time. Instead, she looked at him and smiled warmly,

"And you are even more charming and sweet than in an old people's art show and with a mouth full of pizza."

He squeezed her hand and Genie thought to herself, she wouldn't rather be anywhere else.

Chapter 13

"So . . . ?"

Addie was staring at Genie.

"So what?" Genie replied.

"I wanna know about your date with Carson. Tyler told me he picked you up around two."

Genie nodded and shut her locker door.

"Well, I am so sorry but I don't kiss and tell."

Addie's jaw dropped.

"Oh my gosh! You kissed him! Where?"

"You are not gonna believe this."

Addie walked with Genie as they headed down the hallway.

"Try me," Addie replied.

"Old Miller's ice rink."

"Wow you're right. That's definitely a new one. Wow, you guys are pretty into each other." Genie smiled and looked at her best friend. "Yeah, I guess so. We are going for coffee after school today."

"Oh," Addie sounded disappointed, "I guess that means you and I aren't hanging out later."

Genie gasped.

"We can do it some other time though. Don't worry about it."

Addie sounded convincing but Genie knew she was offended. Genie was glad that it was the end of the day. Tuesdays were her favorite day because she only had three serious classes. The other four were gym, art, music appreciation, and journalism. Though it had been a good day, she was glad it was over. Monday had been dreadfully boring.

As Genie headed for the front door of the building, Addie waved and turned to go in a different direction. Genie pushed the large, wooden door open and stepped into the freezing outside world. Her bag dangled from her shoulder. The sparkled ribbon blew in the wind. Genie was walking down the steps when a small patch of ice threw her off balance. She felt herself falling. She hit the concrete steps with a thump. Her knee began to ache and she could feel blood dripping from her knee. She titled her head back and closed her eyes. She sat on the step holding her right knee. Suddenly a muscular arm was wrapped around her shoulder.

"Holy Crap! What happened?"

Genie couldn't find the words. It hurt too badly.

"Here, I'll help you up. We'll take you to the nurse before she leaves."

When Genie looked over her right shoulder, Carson stared down at her knee.

"How bad does it hurt? One to ten. One being nothing, ten being someone shoot me." Genie giggled through the tears that were now dripping down her cheeks.

"Uh," her voice was now trembling, "About a seven."

His eyes widened. "Oh God, we might have to amputate."

He said lifting her up. He held her in his arms. As Genie looked around and saw that everyone in the courtyard was staring at her, she noticed Tyler standing by his truck watching. When their eyes met, he turned away and got in his truck. Genie disregarded the little moment and returned her attention to Carson who was carrying her back into the building while two freshmen boys held the doors. The students who remained in the hallway, moved aside when Carson passed. Genie looked down at her knee, which was still gushing blood. The tears had stopped but the tears from before had dried to her red cheeks. Carson navigated down the hallway not showing a sign of weakness. When he came to the health room, he used his head to knock on the closed door. The nurse's silhouette moved towards the door in the foggy glass window. She opened the door and peaked her head through the crack between the door and the doorframe.

"Nurse Wilson, we've got an injury here."

Nurse Wilson opened the door and finally saw who was in Carson's arms.

"Oh my, yes, please bring her in."

Carson looked at Genie and brought her a little closer to him, he leaned in and whispered in her ear, "You're gonna be fine, I promise."

She looked at him suddenly conscious of how tired she was. He laid her down on the medical bed.

Carson stared into her eyes, which were now slowly closing,

"Don't leave," she muttered.

"Never," he responded.

As she lay on the bed, her knee and skirt covered with blood, he sat in the chair next to her. He watched and held her hand as the nurse wrapped her knee and lathered disinfectant on Genie's skin. She had fallen asleep and lay lifeless as the nurse finished wrapping her leg.

"I would strongly suggest that she go to the hospital to get some x-rays. Because she is not awake for me to ask her questions, I cannot determine whether or not there is a fracture of her knee cap."

Carson nodded and stood.

"Thank you so much. I'll take care of her."

The nurse nodded and stripped her hands of the latex gloves that had kept them clean and sterile. Carson slid his hands under her frail body. He lifted her and maneuvered out of the health room. Now, there were no students left in the halls. The only sound in the hall was Carson's skateboarding sneakers hitting the floor. He carried her all the way to his car, where he gently laid her in the backseat. She remained asleep as he searched for her cell phone. He found it in her pocket. He pulled out of the parking lot and scrolled through her contacts until he came to one named "Mom." He hit call. It rang a few times before Ellen answered.

"Hello, Genesis."

"No, I'm sorry. Mrs. Anderson, this is Carson Knight. I'm calling from Genie's phone because she slipped on some ice outside of Blakeridge. I took her to the nurse's office and Nurse Wilson urged me to take Genie to the hospital. She fell on her knee but she fell asleep before the nurse could tell if it was broken. I'm on my way to the hospital now. I thought maybe you should meet me there."

Ellen gasped. "I'll be right there."

Before Carson could answer, Mrs. Anderson had hung up. He looked in the rearview mirror and peaked at Genie sleeping. She seemed so peaceful and beautiful but so helpless and weak which scared him. The hospital was about half an hour north of Deal Island. The entire ride was silent and when Carson carried her into the emergency room, the receptionist had asked what his sister's name was.

"No," he replied, "that's actually my girlfriend and her name is Genesis Anderson. She suffered a tough fall. We need some x-rays. Now."

The nurse who was working the desk seemed taken back by how forceful Carson was. He wasn't taking any chances when it came to her getting the care she needed.

"Oh, alright then. I'll be right back."

The heavyset black nurse went back through a set of double doors. He laid Genie across three of the seats in the waiting room. She was still out of it and he was getting worried. Her head was lying across his lap and he was stroking her forehead with his thumb. Her phone was in his pocket still. He reached in and pulled it out. He scrolled through her contacts until he came to Addie. He again, pressed call.

"Hey, Genie, how are things going with Carson?"

Carson chuckled, "Hi, Addie, its Carson."

"Oh," she tried not to sound surprised, "why are you calling me on Gen's phone?"

"Genie fell outside the school. I took her to the hospital but I would think that you'd wanna know that she was hurt."

"Oh my gosh! Did she break anything? Can I talk to her?"

"She's still asleep and she hasn't gotten any x-rays yet. I'll have her call you."

"Thanks Carson. You're a really great guy."

"Oh, thanks."

"Bye," Addie said hanging up.

Just as Carson flipped the phone shut, Ellen rushed in, searching the room for her daughter. Carson stood to greet her.

"Oh my God. Her knee! It's all busted up."

Ellen squealed the words as he inspected her daughter's condition.

"Hi, I don't think we've met."

Carson extended his hand and Ellen looked almost surprised by his comment.

"I'm Carson."

Ellen shook his hand and looked Carson up and down.

"I'm Ellen Anderson. Thank you so much for helping Genesis. She is so careless sometimes."

Carson smiled and looked down at Genie's sleeping face. He thought back to the day at the ice rink. She wasn't careless, but graceful. The nurse approached Ellen and looked at Genie. She was pushing a wheelchair.

"We can take her back for some x-rays now."

Ellen nodded and swallowed hard. Carson slid his arms underneath her body once again. He gently placed her in the wheelchair. The nurse nodded at him and turned the wheelchair around. Ellen followed behind the nurse. Carson sat in the chair in the waiting room. He exhaled and leaned back, letting his head rest on the back of the seat. More than anything, he just wanted to know if she would be okay.

Chapter 14

Genie sat in the passenger seat of her mother's car. Her knee had been freshly wrapped in the hospital. Now, there was white tape and gauze stretching from halfway up her shin, all the way to her lower thigh. Her mother was silent as they drove back from the hospital. The x-rays had said that nothing was broken and that some significant bruising was inevitable. They had given her crutches in case it was hard to walk. It was hard to walk. Genie had only two things on her mind; the excruciating pain in her knee and Carson. He had carried her around the school, waited with her in the health room, driven her to the E.R, and waited there until after she came back from getting x-rays. Ellen had to assure him that it was alright that he leave Genie with her, her mother. Carson didn't listen. When Ellen had gone to get the car, Carson sat with Genie.

He had held her hand and told her, "You look more beautiful with white gauze and medical tape on your knee than you do on the ice, on the dock, or in that awful art center."

Genie had laughed and laid her head on his shoulder. He hugged her and began helping her up. He guided her out to her mother's car. When Ellen pulled away from the circular drive, he stood and watched the car drive away.

Now, Genie was thinking about everything he had done and no matter what he did, she felt more and more for him with each passing moment. Ellen pulled into the driveway. She slammed the door behind her. Genie struggled to get out of her mom's sedan. She hobbled up the two steps to the front door. Inside, Poppy was sitting in his recliner reading the paper.

"Oh, Genesis. You really know how to bang yourself up."

Her grandfather was one of the sweetest men she knew. He still had that old time slang that never left him after the 50's.

"Yeah, I know Poppy. Nothing's broken though."

He nodded, returning to his paper. He remained quiet but her mother did not. Ellen was storming around the kitchen, making all kinds of noise. She was mad but Genie couldn't imagine why. She wobbled into the kitchen and sat in one of the chairs that hadn't been pushed in from breakfast.

"Mom, why are you mad?"

"Genesis! You have got to be more careful!"

Genie was outraged, "How could I help it if there was ice on the steps?!"

Ellen turned around and faced Genie dead on. She was standing across the kitchen but her glare made Genie feel as though she was right in her face.

"I had to miss work because you didn't think to look where you stepped. If I leave my job too often, I'm gonna get fired and we'll be out on the street."

Ellen's face was bright red and there wasn't a drop of compassion in her voice.

"I'm sorry. I know you hate working but we had no choice after dad died," Genie's voice softened and her mother's facial expression changed too.

"Genesis, you have to be careful. I don't know if I can handle losing you too."

Her mom began to cry and it was moments like these that Genie felt closest with her mom. Her mom never acted like a human and when she showed any emotion at all, it was anger towards Genie. Just like on Sunday when she came back from her day with Carson. Genie had gotten lectured by her mother, because she wasn't there to say good-bye to Trinity. That was part of the glory about being out when her sister left. Ellen didn't ask anything about her date, her mother immediately began yelling at her for not being there. That was probably the reason they didn't have a good mother-daughter relationship. Now, Ellen was sobbing and leaning against the counter for support. Genie normally would have gone over to comfort her mother but the pain in her knee was too overwhelming to even think about moving.

"Mom, come here."

Genie held out her arms and her mother hugged her. Ellen pulled up a chair and sat across from Genie at the table.

"So, let's talk. We haven't chatted in a while."

Genie was stunned to hear her mother offer to talk.

"You know, I like Carson. He seems like a nice young man."

Genie was stunned to hear this as well.

"Yeah, he's really funny. Surprisingly, he's a bit of a romantic."

Genie chuckled as the words came out. Ellen smiled, "He seems to care about you." Genie nodded.

"How are Tyler and Addie?"

Genie's thoughts about Carson were interrupted by her mother's question.

"Uh, they seem to be fine. Tyler and Lindsey broke up."

"Oh, that's unfortunate."

Genie nodded and took an apple out of the bowl of fruit that sat in the middle of the table. "He didn't seem too upset. I don't think he loved her."

"Well, Genesis, love is a very strong word. I don't think it's possible for anyone your age to 'fall in love.'"

Ellen said 'fall in love' as though she was saying something about a dead family member. Genie wasn't sure what she thought about what her mom said.

"You could be right. I don't know. I've never had an experience with love."

It was more of a thought in Genie's head that just seemed to spill out into words.

Ellen replied, "You have come across love, just not the romantic kind. You love your sister and brother. You love Tyler and Addie like you love Noah and Trinity. You love to write. You love your school. You experience love everyday, you just have never been in love."

Genie thought hard about what her mother said. She did love Noah, Addie, and Tyler. They were her brothers and sister. She couldn't quite bring herself to say that she loved Trinity. Genie took a bite of the green apple.

"Thanks mom."

Ellen nodded and waved as Genie tried to stand from her seat.

"Good night."

"Good night, Genesis."

The pain increased with every step and she wasn't quite sure that she could make it up the steps.

"Noah! Can you help me?"

Genie called upstairs from the bottom of the steps. Noah looked down and his eyes grew bigger.

"What happened?"

His voice was high pitched and excited.

"I fell at school. It hurts really bad and I need your help getting up the steps."

Noah nodded and ran down the steps to help his big sister. He stood on the step just staring at her knee.

"Ok, you can help by letting me put my arm around your shoulder and keeping me balanced. Okay?"

Noah nodded and did exactly as she said. He guided her up the steps and helped her onto her bed.

"Thanks, Noah."

Noah smiled widely and left. Genie lay on her bed, staring at her blue ceiling. She wanted to call Addie and tell her everything that had happened. When she reached into her pocket for her phone, she felt nothing. Where was her phone? Had she left it at the hospital? Had it dropped out of her pocket when she fell? She couldn't do anything about it now; she'd have to look for it tomorrow. Genie glanced down at her skirt. It had a little blood around the bottom. Disgusting, she thought. She went to her dresser and pulled out some pajama pants. She changed and went back to staring at the ceiling. Carson ran through her mind.

Carson sat on his bed, staring out the window. This evening had been very interesting and he was happy to be able to relax. When he had come home from the hospital with some blood on his uniform shirt, his mother had been curious.

"Hey, Car, where you been?"

"You know that girl, Genie, well she fell outside of the school and busted her knee. I took her to the hospital."

Veronica, Carson's mom, had leaned against the kitchen counter looking surprised.

"You really like this girl, don't you?" she asked.

Carson and his mom were close but they never had talked about any of his former girlfriends and they weren't going to start now. He shook his head and walked down the hall to his room. His house was one floor and it was on the smaller side. His home in Washington D.C had been a small apartment in a bad neighborhood. The cost of living in the city was really high and even though his mom had a good job, it still wasn't enough to make ends meet. Veronica wanted to move in the middle of the year because she thought it would be a little easier and when she got the job at a law firm in the town next to Deal Island, she knew it was the right time to do the right thing—move. Carson hadn't really fought with his mom about moving because towards the end of his time in D.C, he really didn't like how his life was playing out. He didn't have many interests and his friends were beginning to get into drugs and a few serious fights had broken out since the beginning of the year and he didn't want to be around it all. When his mom said they were moving, Carson was a little relieved to be getting away from the violence and drugs. Now that he was here on Deal Island, he was happy they had moved. He'd found an amazing girl and made a few decent friends. He liked the small town and he liked his new house. He had a view of the water from his window. Carson stared at the waves when something in his pocket vibrated. He reached into the pocket of his khaki uniform pants.

He had forgotten to give Genie her phone and now someone was calling. Carson flipped the phone open.

"Hello?" Carson asked.

The voice on the other line was that of another guy.

"Who is this?" The other voice asked.

"Uh this is Carson Knight. Who is this?"

"Tyler Moore. Where's Genie?"

"Oh, sorry man, she left her phone with me by accident. This afternoon was a little crazy."

"Yeah, is she okay?"

Carson had no problem talking about Genie. It all came with ease.

"Yeah, we went to the hospital and she got some x-rays. Nothing's broken but her knee is pretty messed up. There's gonna be a lot of bruising and I swear, her knee bled for easily 20 minutes."

Carson chuckled but Tyler didn't make a sound.

"Yeah," he replied, "well, I'm glad she's okay. Thanks for the info, Carson."

"No problem, man. Have a good night."

When Tyler hung up, Carson flipped the phone shut. Tyler seemed awfully tense and Carson couldn't really picture such an outgoing person like Genie, spending time with a quiet and uptight guy like Tyler. Carson returned his gaze to the waves. He couldn't really picture himself without Genie.

Chapter 15

"Oh, so are we on for tonight?"

Addie was driving Genie back to the Anderson house.

"I can't. Carson and I are going out tonight. Sorry."

From the passenger seat, Genie could see Addie rolling her blue eyes.

"Okay. Just thought I'd ask."

Genie knew she had to change the subject.

"So, how are things going with Aidan?"

Addie's expression softened.

"Good, the only reason we aren't doing anything tonight is because he's visiting Salisbury this weekend. He's really looking forward to going there next year."

Salisbury University was a good school and Genie was happy to hear that Aidan's future looked bright.

"That's good. Are you and Tyler just gonna chill at the house?"

Addie nodded as she turned the car onto Genie's street.

"All right well, call me when you get back from your date with Dr. McDreamy."

Genie laughed.

"Will do. Thanks for the ride. Bye."

"Anytime. Bye!"

Genie waved to Addie as she slowly got out of the car. They had taken the bandages off of her knee a few days ago. Her knee had swollen up like a balloon that had been inflated before a birthday party. It was blue, black, and a little yellow. It looked gross but there was nothing she could do. It was healing.

She turned and faced the house. The light yellow house was dark which meant that Poppy had taken her car to get something from the store.

In a few minutes, the bus would drop Noah off at the end of the street along with all the other neighborhood kids. Genie would meet him by the corner and walk him back to the house. Whenever Genie wasn't home, Poppy walked him back. It was the job of whoever was home at the time of drop off.

Genie slid the key into the door and unlocked it. She set down her bag by the door. She jogged up the stairs to her room. Her alarm clock said it was 3:46. That meant that in one hour and 14 minutes, Carson would pick her up and they'd go out.

Genie glanced into the mirror. Her hair looked terrible and there was a zit on her chin. Great. She turned towards her closet and slid the door to the left on its track. Inside, her best pieces hung, waiting to be picked. She sorted through half the closet before she found what she wanted. It was a purple sweater and a gray sparkled tank top was hung inside of it. She would wear blue jeans and boots along with the sweater and shirt. She'd probably curl her hair . . . or maybe straighten it. Just as possible hairstyles were making their way around her mind, the front door slammed and Genie jumped at the noise. Noah.

She rushed down the stairs to find Noah laying on the floor sobbing. He was in the fetal position and his little body shook with his sobs. Genie ran to his side and pulled him off of the floor and into her arms. She sat down next to him and held and rocked him.

He sobbed for a few minutes before Genie dared to ask, "What's wrong?"

He looked up at her, his cheeks pink and tears streaming down his face.

"I miss dad!"

He said, choking on his words. Genie's heart broke. It was very rare that Noah talked about dad and when he did, he would break down just as he was doing now. Genie's eyes became heavy and she could feel her own tears coming to the surface.

"I know, we all do. But it'll be okay."

She reassured him, stroking his head.

"No, it won't! He's dead. He is never coming back and he can't come to my class and talk about his job on career day like all the other dads."

Genie felt something inside her die with his angry and disappointed words.

"Oh, Noah. I know this is tough. I know."

Noah's body shook hard and Genie couldn't help but cry. She didn't know how to comfort him. She dealt with the same grief that he did. After four years, the things they would have to go through without their dad still brought the family to tears. Noah didn't have his dad for Career Day, or the pine-box derby. Trinity had to go off to college without saying goodbye to her dad unlike all of her classmates. Even though Trinity seemed invincible, she used to spend nights crying in her room. Genie often thought about how he wouldn't walk her down the isle or dance with her on her wedding day.

Noah's cries of grief only brought back these solemn thoughts.

"Shh, don't worry. It'll work out."

Genie leaned back and stroked his back. More than ever, Genie wanted her dad. He was a strong man that had no fear and he always knew the right things to say.

Genie thought in her head, *Dad, tell me what to say. Just tell me what to do. I miss you so much. I need you. We need you.* Genie knew in her heart that she wouldn't get an answer but she replayed that in her head, begging for an answer.

After 20 minutes on the hard, wood floor, Genie carried Noah to his room. His room had sports memorabilia covering the walls and shelves. He had trophies from all the different things he participated in.

Noah stopped crying, instead he just gasped for air. Genie laid him on his unmade bed. She covered him with a blanket. She turned but when she got to the door, she turned around and watched as his eyelids slowly closed over his glassy blue eyes. Genie went to her room and sat on her bed.

She needed to clean herself up so that she'd be ready for her date with Carson. She hadn't told him about her father's death, or anything deep for that matter. Maybe tonight she would let it all out. Maybe she wouldn't. She changed into the sweater and jeans. Usually when she got ready, she had music playing from the radio but not today. She got ready in silence. She didn't want to wake Noah up but another part of her just needed the quiet so that she could relax and enjoy the calm that came after the storm. She could hear someone coming in the door downstairs. Her mother was probably getting home from work. Which meant it was around five. Crap. Carson would be getting here any minute.

"Genesis, Noah, where are you guys?"

Genie ran down the stairs and held her index finger over her mouth. Ellen raised an eyebrow in a 'you-did-not-just-shoosh-your-mother' way.

Genie whispered to her, "Noah's sleeping. He had a rough day."

Genie could have told her about her brother's breakdown but why cause her mother even more stress.

"Carson is gonna be here soon."

Ellen nodded and walked to the kitchen. She had bags of groceries hanging from her wrists. Genie was about to turn and go back upstairs when she saw Carson pull up. He got out and shut his car door. Genie knew that he would ring the bell, which would inevitably wake Noah. She carefully opened and shut the door. He was walking up the path to the porch and when he saw her, he grinned and his eyes darted from her feet to her face.

"Hey, how you doin?" He said as he approached the porch.

Genie still had one hand on the door handle.

"Why don't you come in? I have to grab something. You have to be super quiet. My little brother is sleeping and it might get bad if we wake him up."

Carson nodded and bit his bottom lip. Genie opened the door and they both entered the warm house.

"Can I see him?"

Genie was shocked to hear Carson ask this.

"You want to see my little brother?" Carson nodded.

Genie shrugged and led him up the stairs. He steadied her as she hobbled up the steps. She slowly opened the door to Noah's room. She stood with her back to the doorframe. Carson entered and stood next to her. Genie watched as her brother slept. He was really a good kid. He looked so innocent and precious as he slept. Carson grabbed her hand. She looked up at him and they both smiled. Genie held his hand and led him out of the narrow doorframe. He followed her as she walked to her room. She let go of his hand so that she could walk across her room to get her purse. He stood in the doorframe and looked around her room.

When Genie grabbed his hand and led him out the doorway, she noticed just how big his hands were. They both walked down the steps and stopped at the front door. Genie didn't say anything to her mother before they left; instead, she simply waved. When they got outside, Carson wrapped his arms around her and kissed her right in front of her house. When they stopped, Genie looked at him and asked,

"What was that for?"

He smiled and answered, "Well I thought it would be awkward in front of your little brother."

Genie laughed and they walked to his car.

"So where are we off to today?"

Carson got into the driver's seat and Genie slipped into the passenger seat.

"Well," he said pulling out of the driveway, "I thought maybe you'd like to go to a fancy shmancy dinner."

"You thought correct."

They both laughed. When Carson pulled up to DeLuca's Italian Restaurant, Genie was shocked. De Luca's was where her parents used to go for their anniversary dinners. She did not expect Carson to take her anywhere this nice. Carson was definitely a romantic one but he was the spontaneous kind.

He didn't seem like the type of guy who took his girls to fancy restaurants. He must have suspected her surprise and turned towards her.

"Well, are you a little surprised?" he asked.

Genie nodded and chuckled.

"I've learned to expect the unexpected with you. But I am very happy," she said opening the door.

Carson held the door open for her and she walked into the dimly lit restaurant. Inside, a man in a suit was standing by a podium.

"Hello, do you have a reservation?"

Carson nodded and replied, "It should be under Knight."

"Ahh, yes, right this way Mr. Knight," instructed the host.

Carson turned around and smiled at Genie.

She raised her eyebrows, "Mr. Knight. It has a nice ring."

Carson smiled and turned around to follow the waiter. He led them to a table by a window. The restaurant overlooked the bay. The table had a white tablecloth; there were two plates at each place setting. There were two forks, a spoon, two different types of knives and a cloth napkin on top of the plates. The waiter pulled out a chair and gestured for Genie to sit. She sat and thanked him. Carson took his seat across from her. There was a lit candle in between them, which blocked her view of him. He quickly fixed that, moving the candle towards the window. Genie and Carson held hands on the table. When a different waiter came to their table and asked what they wanted to drink, Carson replied,

"We'll take a bottle of your finest red wine."

When the waiter cleared his throat and put his hands on his hips, Carson quickly replied, "I was kidding sir, I'm sorry. Could we have two diet cokes? Thank you."

The waiter turned away, clearly disgusted by Carson's sense of humor.

"You would be the one to get kicked out of restaurant for asking for alcohol. That's bad."

Genie told him after the waiter wasn't in earshot.

He returned that with, "Which is just the way you like it."

Genie couldn't think of a comeback for his snappy comment. He was clever and she couldn't beat him. She squeezed his hands and he smiled, the dimples appearing again.

"So you wanna know a little about me?" Genie said rolling her shoulders.

"That's kind of why I'm dating you." Carson said. Genie laughed before continuing, "Well, something I haven't told you is that my dad died four years ago."

Carson looked down, "I am so sorry, Genie. Its cool if you don't wanna talk about it."

"No, it's fine. I wanna talk to you about it. He was an amazing man. He really was. When I was almost ten, he got diagnosed with cancer. We were scared. He was the core of the family and no one knew what would happen if he died. He was a doctor and to see him so helpless really broke my family's heart. We were so devastated. He fought it and for a while, it looked good. He went through chemotherapy but it didn't help much, the cancer came back and when I was 12, he died. My mom went into mourning and she sat in her room and cried every night for around two months. He was the love of her life. I didn't even know if she'd ever be able to move on. It was really bad."

Carson squeezed her hands. Not one tear came.

She grinned and continued, "Whenever my dad died, it was on the cover of the town's newspaper and I remember reading what they said about him and thinking that there was so much they didn't say. So I want to change that from now on. That's why I like to write so much."

Carson looked impressed by what she had said, "That's pretty cool. You sound like you have a plan. That's cool."

She inhaled.

"I was really close with my dad. We were inseparable and I even look like him. Well, when he died, my mom didn't even speak to me. It was like I was the one that had killed him. She still isn't all that friendly with me. It's weird. I don't know what to do to make it better. I want to be close with her because she's the only parent I have left but I just don't know what to do. People say it's a phase and that I'm just a normal teenager and that I'll get along better with her later but I just don't know. I think it might be her, not me."

"People say everything I do is a phase. He likes art. It's a phase. He plays hockey. It's a phase. He doesn't like peas. It's a phase. Not everything is a phase. I doubt I'll ever like peas. I think they're pretty nasty. Some of it's just the way you are. I don't know when adults are going to start understanding that teenagers aren't ticking time bombs about to go off on an emotional rant. Believe it or not, some of us are mature."

Genie laughed at his tangent. It was true. Adults never did seem to understand that teenagers are real people, not these extracts of adults that are slopped together to make an emotional, angry, and anxious mess. Some have self-control.

"I think I'm with you on that one, Car," she said.

After a little while, the waiter came back with their food. Genie had ordered fettuccini alfredo and Carson, the baked ziti. They ate slowly, talking a little bit in between bites.

Finally, Genie asked, "What should I know about you?"

Carson put down his fork.

"Well," he said linking his hands on the tabletop, "I murdered a man. I'm just kidding. I grew up in a house in the suburbs. My mom and dad were completely opposite people and that was part of the reason they got divorced. My mom was an eccentric artist who was creative and unique. My dad was a by-the-book businessman. He was a workaholic and he made quite a chunk of change. When they separated, my mom took Landon and I to her new apartment in D.C. My dad wasn't pleased. When the court date came, we were sitting in the courtroom and uh, the judge said that we both would be better off with our dad but when I saw the horror on my mom's face, I couldn't do it. I told the judge that I wanted to live with my mom. The judge said that my dad would be able to financially support my brother and I, but I said no. I wanted to live with my mom. My dad looked so mad. I knew that he wasn't disappointed, but angry. I made him look bad. He had all the money in the world but that couldn't buy love from his son. I didn't like him. I still don't. He hasn't talked to me since. Once and a while he used to come to the apartment and threaten my mom. He'd tell her that he, uh, wanted her back and that she was nothing without him. He said that she'd come crawling back but she never did and he couldn't and still can't handle that. So yeah, that's my story."

Genie had taken her hand from his and she covered her mouth.

"Your mom sounds like really strong. I'd love to meet her."

Carson nodded and took her hand again, "Yeah and she really wants to meet you. I'll take you to my house sometime."

"Well, you know how I feel about my mom," Genie said staring at her hands.

"You know," Carson said, "I think she loves you more than you know."

"And why do you say that?" Genie asked

"You didn't see her face when she rushed into the hospital. You were asleep. She was so scared, Gen."

Carson spoke with such gentleness about her mother. Genie looked out at the waves and willed herself not to cry. Hearing someone say that her mom cared about her and was worried when she fell made Genie feel loads better. Her mom had never showed any affection toward her. Ellen and Trinity were always so close and Genie and Victor had been until his death. Genie had always known that her mother loved her but she knew it was because a mother has to love her children. It was human nature. It never occurred to her that Ellen loved her in a way that was personal or in a unique way. Genie could feel a tear drip down her cheek. Carson reached over the table and used his thumb to wipe the tear from her face.

He whispered in her ear.

"You are even more stunning with a single tear running down your cheek than with gauze on your knee, or ice in your hair, sitting on the pier, or in an awful art show."

Genie smiled at him and everything about her mother faded away. How was she supposed to answer that anyway?

"Thanks, I really appreciate it, but, you're really cheesy."

It sounded dorky but he smiled. Genie was here, with Carson, right now and that was all that mattered. Right now was all that counted.

Chapter 16

"Why are you here?"

Trinity stood over Genie. She sat on the second to last stair and watched Trinity roll her eyes.

"Well, I drove down because I had an announcement and I wanted to tell you guys in person."

Trinity was standing in front of the fireplace at the Anderson house. Poppy was in his brown recliner, Ellen on the other end of the couch. Noah was on Genie's lap. Trinity had driven down after her last class on Friday afternoon. Unfortunately, she had been there when Genie had arrived back from her date with Carson. Now, Trinity had gathered the entire family together.

"Okay, well as you all know, I am studying to be involved in teaching and I am very interested in taking part in world studies . . ."

"Oh dear, just tell us already!"

Ellen said, her voice bursting with anticipation and excitement.

"I have been selected to go to Indonesia this semester!"

Trinity couldn't get the words out fast enough.

"Oh Trinity!" Ellen squealed and rose to hug her daughter.

"What is this for?"

"Well," Trinity explained, "it's part of a special program to help children learn math. Math is the same all over the world, and I've always wanted to travel, so I applied. And I was accepted."

Ellen looked at Trinity, not even acknowledging the other people in the room.

"When do you leave?" Ellen had a million questions.

Trinity took a seat on the couch as her mother stood staring at her, "Well, I have to give them my decision in three weeks."

"Your decision on what?"

Poppy asked sitting up in his chair.

"Whether I want to go," Trinity said.

"Why wouldn't you want to go?"

Ellen sounded more concerned than questioning.

"I don't know, but they like to give the students time to think it over and talk with their families about it."

"Well," Ellen said straightening her back, "we want you to go."

Genie sat and watched all of this drama unfold in her very own living room. A few months with no contact from Trinity sounded better and better with each passing moment. Noah looked at Genie and raised an eyebrow. He was a smart kid and he knew just as well as she did that their mother would lose it when it was time for Trinity to go.

It was late and Genie wanted to go to bed. Her date was amazing but it had worn her out and she was ready to get some rest.

"Well, I'm gonna go ahead to bed. Congrats sis, I'm sure it'll be cool." She said excusing herself.

Trinity looked almost shocked and offended by what Genie said.

"Uh, thanks. It will be cool."

Genie made a break for her room, leaving her family behind. When she got to her room, she called Addie.

"Hello?"

"Hey, Ads, its Genie."

"Oh, hey how was your Knight in shining armor. You see how I worked that in there?" Genie chuckled. Addie worked his name into the conversation as much as she could.

"So romantic. As always."

Addie laughed.

"Well, it's a good thing he didn't make any plans for you guys for tomorrow because I got us tickets to go to see this play in,"

"Wait, we had plans for tomorrow?"

Addie grew angry, "Yeah, we did. I'm getting pretty sick of you blowing me off for this guy. I mean I'm happy that he's so great and all but don't forget your friends."

With that, the line went dead. Addie hung up and Genie threw her phone onto her bed. She slid down the side of her bed. Her hands covered her face. She sat on the floor leaning against her bed, cupping her face in her hands. Having Addie mad at her upset her. Addie was her best friend and they were close. Why does it matter if Genie missed a few plans? Why couldn't Addie just be happy for her? It was obvious that Addie was jealous and that was why she was being so irrational about the whole thing. Genie picked up her phone and dialed Carson.

"Yellow?" Carson joked as he answered the phone.

"Hey, it's me."

"Hey, good looking, what's up?" Genie blushed.

"We're still on for tomorrow, right?"

Carson's voice was perfect on the other end, "Absolutely, I'll meet you at the pier at three. I gotta pick up my car so it'd be easier for me to meet you there."

"Okay, I'll ask Trinity to drive me on her way out of town."

"Alrighty then, I'll see you tomorrow."

"Bye," Genie said.

"Bye," he said hanging up.

The idea of Trinity driving her anywhere was scary but Genie had been using up more gas than usual and she didn't have much more money to spend on gas. The pier they had sat on when they first went out was about a 20-minute drive from her house. She liked the old pier that didn't serve boats anymore. It was a place that they could go to relax and whether or not things worked out between her and Carson, she'd still visit the pier. Tomorrow was gonna be great, she could tell. Genie lay on her bed and watched the trees blow outside her window. She thought about Carson and how she couldn't imagine the world going on without him.

Chapter 17

"I am leaving in five minutes, whether you're in my car or not."
Trinity screamed to the entire house.

Genie didn't know why her sister had to be such a bitch when it came to doing people favors. Genie sat at the kitchen table while she could hear everyone moving around upstairs. Noah came down the stairs and stood in front of Genie. He held up his hands and pressed down three fingers on one hand.

"Seven days until the pine-box derby," Noah said.

He was so excited about the pine-box derby. He had his pine-box car thing in the garage and Tyler came over every Saturday or Sunday after church, to work on it with Noah.

"Are you excited?"

Genie asked already knowing the answer. Noah nodded energetically.

"You're gonna come right?" Noah asked.

"Wouldn't miss it for the world," Genie said giving Noah a high five.

Trinity exploded into the room. You could tell that she was stressed.
She looked straight at Genie and screamed, "Let's go!"

"Okay!" Genie said getting up from her chair.

Trinity stomped through the kitchen and living room. She swung open the front door. Genie climbed in her sister's car. When Trinity turned the car on, the time read 3:03.

"Oh, we gotta go. I'm gonna be late," Genie said buckling her seat belt.

Trinity glared at her, "Do you honestly think I care?"

Genie rolled her eyes and looked out the passenger window. Neither of the girls spoke until Genie was telling her to stop the car.

"Thanks for the ride," Genie said getting out of the car.

"You're welcome."

Her sister sped off. Genie had no idea what was wrong with her. Trinity was rarely late for anything and if she was, it wasn't her fault. So for Trinity to be rushing was a sight all in itself. Where she was rushing to was a completely different set of questions.

Genie walked down the hill and saw that no one was standing at the pier waiting. He was probably on his way. It was pretty cold but not freezing. The skies were gray and showed sign of snow. It wasn't cold enough to snow but it was hard to imagine rain in late March. Genie sat on the edge of the pier and let her legs hangs over the water. The waves tossed violently below her feet. Genie checked her phone for a time. It was 3:27. He was pretty late. Genie texted him: Hey, I'm at the pier. I'll c u soon? She waited a few minutes but nothing. Her inbox had no new messages. She was getting a little cold. She checked the time again 3:44. Had he came and then left? She scrolled through her contacts to 'C.' It rang about five times before his voicemail took over.

"Hey, this is Carson. Leave a message. Bye."

Genie waited until after the beep, "Hey, I'm here and you're not. Give me a call."

She swung her legs and watched as a bird flew across the water. She took her phone out and played one of the free games that came on most phones. After beating her high score, she checked the time again. It was 4:08. He was supposed to be here over an hour ago. Genie was shifting her position when she heard the slightest rumble. Just as she looked at the sky, a drop of water fell right below her eye. Then she felt another on her right arm. One by one, the raindrops fell. Before she knew it, the rain poured down. Now, she really wanted to go home. She wished that she had driven herself there. She had no ride home and it was near an hour walk. Genie could feel the tears welling up. Why hadn't he come? Maybe he didn't want to see her again. Did he not want to see her at all? What had she done wrong? She wanted to go home and not have to deal with anyone ever again. How could he do this to her? How embarrassing. She was so ashamed. She had fell for it. She trusted him. How could he? Genie couldn't control the tears that streamed down her face. Her mascara was running down the sides of her face. She didn't want to call her mom to pick her up. Ellen wouldn't understand. Addie was mad at her. Trinity was long gone. It would be embarrassing for Poppy to pick her up. Genie felt her cell phone ringing in her pocket. She reached for it then flipped it open,

"Hello?" Her voice trembled.

"Hey, does Noah still want me to come over, we can't paint it in the rain."

"Tyler?!" Genie broke down and sobbed.

"Genie, what's wrong? Where are you?"

His voice sounded concerned and scared.

"Can you pick me up at the old dock behind the bait shop?" Genie asked with all of the hope in the world that Tyler would be the cool friend she had always known.

"I'll be right there." He reassured her.

He hung up and so did Genie. She felt her legs growing weak. She knelt down on the hard wood dock. She was freezing and wet. Her heart was broken. She cupped her face in her hands. She sobbed up until she felt Tyler's arms around her.

"It'll be okay."

She was a little scared when he surprised her. She hadn't heard him coming.

"Shhhhh, it'll be fine."

He held her and rocked her gently. She continued to sob. He lifted her up and walked her up the muddy hill to his car. Inside, there was a blanket on the passenger seat waiting for her. She wrapped it around herself. She sat staring at the windshield as he drove through the pouring rain. They didn't talk until he pulled into the Anderson driveway.

"Thank you."

Tyler shook his head, "No problem. Tell Noah that we'll spray paint his car tomorrow."

Genie stepped out of the truck. Tyler was pulling out when Genie knocked on the glass window. He rolled the window down.

She couldn't say anything before he spoke, "Don't let anyone break your heart. This is gonna sound really stupid and cheesy but I just did a research paper on her so go with me. Eleanor Roosevelt said, 'No one can make you feel bad without your permission.' Don't let him make you feel bad. I know it's corny but just believe me."

With that, Tyler rolled up the window and backed out of the driveway. Genie stood in the same spot and watched him go. She was still wrapped in the blanket and she watched him leave as the rain poured down around her.

Genie walked into the house. Her clothes were drenched and she was shivering uncontrollably. Poppy was sitting in his recliner when she entered. He stood and his eyes grew wide.

"Genie, I'm gonna get you some tea and a blanket. Go put dry clothes on this minute."

He sounded serious and in control but she knew that he was worried and curious. She walked up the stairs and prayed that Noah wouldn't see her. She really wasn't strong enough to answer his questions right now. Even if she did explain, Noah wouldn't understand why she had stood there as long as she did and he wouldn't get why it hurt her so much that Carson didn't show. Luckily, Noah had the radio on and the music drowned out the sounds of her footsteps. His door was closed and it didn't seem like he would be out of his room anytime soon. Genie walked into her room. She stared at her reflection in the mirror. Mascara was running down her face and her hair was a mess. It was wavy from being wet and her clothes stuck to her body. Her blue fleece hung off of her and her jeans looked like they were skintight. She suddenly felt ten pounds heavier than before. She stripped off each layer and changed into her warmest sweat pants. She slipped on a T-shirt and school hoodie. She removed her wet socks and slipped into her favorite pink fur slippers. She brushed through her wet hair and put it up in a ponytail. She was already feeling a little better. She held the banister and trotted down the stairs. Poppy was sitting on the couch. On the coffee table were two steaming mugs. Genie smiled and took a seat on the couch next to her grandfather. He picked up one of the mugs and handed it to her. Genie sipped the burning tea and set down the cup.

"I knew from the start that he wasn't a nice boy."

Poppy stared at her. His comment broke her heart. How did her grandfather pick up on this stuff when she was oblivious?

"I don't know what happened."

Poppy put down his mug and exhaled.

"Well," he began, "I think that sometimes, getting into a relationship with someone seems like a good idea at first but some boys aren't mature enough to handle you."

Genie thought about what he said before answering.

"Poppy, he seemed perfect. I don't know what went wrong."

"Well, I can assure you that it had nothing to do with you. It was a personal problem. I'm pretty sure."

Genie brought her knees to her chest.

He continued, "You should talk to your mother. She had all kinds of boy problems when she was your age."

Genie was stunned. She had never thought about her mother as a child. She sure didn't think about Ellen dating. Her mother wasn't the partying and teen angst type of person. She seemed more like the person who was born with a career plan and with her personality found already.

Genie replied, "I never thought about that."

Poppy nodded and put down his mug.

"O yes. She had terrible taste in boys."

Genie laughed out loud and Poppy smiled turned and smiled at her.

"Yes, your mother was quite the rebel."

Genie could feel her mouth drop open. Her mother . . . a rebel. The two seemed as close as Hitler and a priest.

"You're kidding?"

"Oh no, she was quite a handful. She would come home at all hours of the night. She even got a tattoo one time."

Genie was shocked. She leaned back in the couch and laughed.

"What did you do?"

Poppy shook his head.

"I think I screamed for hours. She of course, didn't speak to your grandmother or I for a week or so."

Genie thought about what the tattoo might have been of. Was it a skull and cross bones? What if it was some guy's name?

"Well, after a year or two and a night in jail, your mother straightened up."

A night in jail! This got better and better. Her mother in a jail cell was something that Genie couldn't dream up in a million years. Genie burst out laughing at the thought of her now suburbanized mother sitting in a jail cell with a plate of lasagna set on her lap.

"She really changed when she met your father."

Genie's smile faded and her thoughts turned to a younger version of her father.

"Yes," Poppy continued, "he didn't smoke, drink, and he had inkless skin."

Genie laughed trying to fight tears.

"I remember," he said, "when your grandmother and I were trying to select a name for your mother. We went through hundreds of names before your grandmother thought of the perfect name."

"Ellen?" Genie said.

Poppy frowned, "Your mother's name isn't Ellen. It's Eleanor."

Genie had never heard her mother been called Eleanor in her entire life.

"Why did you choose Eleanor?"

"Because we knew that your mother would be a strong woman. Eleanor Roosevelt was an incredible woman and we knew that with a name like that, your mother would have someone strong to look up to."

"Wow, that's really special," Genie said, putting down her mug.

"I don't think my mom and dad thought about picking a name with a meaning. I know my name is religious and all but . . ." Genie trailed off.

"Oh, Genie! Your name has so much meaning!"

"It does?"

"Oh, yes. When you were born, you were very sick. Your mother was worried that you were not going to make it past the beginning of your life. They were so worried."

Genie listened as he explained,

"So they named you Genesis which means beginning or birth, in a hope that you would make it past the beginning. They hoped that your beginning would be the most troublesome part of your life."

Genie stopped and thought. She had never thought about her mother being worried about her. Ellen always seemed so caught up with Trinity. Genie tried to imagine her mother and father standing over an incubator as Genie struggled to hold onto life. It seemed like her mother really wanted her. Not that Genie thought that she didn't want her, it just seemed like now she understood the way her mom cared about her.

"When your father died," Poppy thought about his words before continuing, "Eleanor was so strong. It may not seem that way to you, but she dealt with his death fairly well. He was the love of her life and when she spoke about him, her face would light up. She was so strong while he was sick. When he died, she finally got to grieve. Compared to the way she could have dealt with the situation, she was the best mother you could ask for."

Genie tried to hold back her tears.

Genie remembered visiting her dad in the hospital and she tried to imagine what her mother must have been feeling while her children stood by her husbands bed asking when he would be all better. Then it occurred to Genie, Trinity was the only child that was old enough when he was sick, to understand the situation. Trinity knew what Ellen was feeling and what she and Victor were going through. Genie and Noah were too young. They thought their dad was going to get better. They were waiting for him to come home and for things to go back to normal. They never did. Trinity probably supported Ellen when things got tough. Now Genie understood why Trinity and her mother were so close. They were all each other had. Suddenly, Genie understood a lot more about her mother and sister. Poppy smiled and Genie hugged him, holding him tight.

"Thank you so much, Poppy. That really helped."

He looked at her and smiled, "I knew it would."

He winked and grabbed his paper, returning to his reading.

Chapter 18

The days that followed the afternoon on the pier were different than the weeks leading up to it. Genie dismissed Carson. She didn't need him. She told Addie,

"I don't need to worry about someone who's gonna treat me like that. I'm just worrying about me right now."

She focused on writing and on the paper. She had started a dramatic short story and her thoughts became consumed with perfecting it. She poured her heart and soul into the three—page adventure. It kept her busy and when she showed Mr. Abrams, he was very impressed.

Genie missed Carson a lot. She tried not to think about how he'd hurt her or how she had started to fall for him. It was all in the past. She was beginning to think that she loved him but his standing her up showed that he didn't feel the same. She wasn't going to let herself get hurt again. She was independent. She didn't need a guy to make her feel good.

She didn't go back to hanging out with Addie and Tyler as she did before. Genie just worried about herself. She got a haircut and got her nails done. It was her time to focus on being herself.

Genie walked down the halls of Blakeridge, her expression dull. The day seemed to last forever. She didn't see Carson in the halls but she'd seen Tyler and Addie. Tyler had been understanding and he didn't mention what happened on Saturday. Addie was a little tougher but she seemed to loosen up and forgive Genie for anything that had happened in the past couple weeks.

Now, Genie was walking to lunch. She planned on sitting with Addie and Tyler, obviously not Carson. The cafeteria was crowded and the noise level was high. The formal looking dining area was filled with the chatter of the students of Blakeridge. The smell of spaghetti sauce enveloped Genie as she entered through the two large doors. She saw Addie sitting at a round table. She waved and motioned to the seat next to her. Genie smiled and waved. Genie was heading toward the table but she was also searching for Carson. She didn't necessarily want a confrontation but she did want to know if he was present. She didn't see him. Genie took a seat in the wooden chair next to Addie.

"Hey, how were classes?"

Genie looked to Addie as she asked.

"Oh they seemed kinda long. What about you?"

"They were okay I guess. I wonder where Tyler is?"

Genie looked around the large room. Out of the corner of her eye, she saw Tyler's blackish brown hair. Just as Genie looked to see him, he was walking up to a group of guys. Genie watched as Tyler tapped the shoulder of a guy who's back was to her. The guy, who Tyler had tapped, turned around. Carson.

Genie screamed, "Tyler, no!"

Tyler brought back his arm. Carson had no time to react before Tyler's fist hit him between the eyes. It all seemed to happen in slow motion as Genie watched. She suddenly felt light headed. Tyler shook his hand in the air as one of the guys that had been standing with Carson examined him on the ground.

Genie leapt to her feet and ran through the room. She weaved in and out of tables and dodged passing students. The room grew silent and every student looked to wear Carson was lying on the ground, his hands covering his face. Genie knelt by Carson's distraught body. She tapped his bicep, "Carson, it's me. Look at me."

Carson moved his hands from in front of his face. The bridge of his nose was already beginning to bruise. Blood was gushing from his nose. Genie's eyes sagged at the gruesome sight. He looked as though he was in so much pain, physically and emotionally. Genie looked up at Tyler who looked smugly pleased. How could he be happy causing someone pain? He smiled at Genie. She was disgusted with him.

"How could you?" Genie accused.

Tyler looked stunned than angry. He turned and sped through the doors of the cafeteria and out the room. Genie looked down at Carson. People had created a circle around him and Genie. Half of the people in the lunchroom had encircled them. Genie had one hand on Carson's solid and defined bicep. His hands were covering his nose. Blood was now on his uniform collar. Genie's fingers stroked his hands. She ran her hand through his short hair. Everyone was watching them but there was so much she wanted to say, so much she wanted to ask. He lifted his head and his eyes caught hers.

"I'm sorry," he muttered.

Genie's heart melted. She knew then and there that she may not need him in her life but she wanted him. She was about to speak when a teacher burst through the wall of students.

Mr. Landers was screaming, "Back up! Back up! Everyone away! Who is responsible?"

An unrecognizable girl's voice came from the back of the pack of students.

"Tyler Moore. He just left."

Mr. Landers turned and the students parted. He stormed out of the cafeteria. Now, the students were disbanding. There was nothing more to see and they didn't want to miss too much of their lunch. Addie emerged, looked at Carson lying on the hardwood floor, then turned and left. There was a look of horror on her face.

Carson began to try to stand. Genie steadied him with her small arm. He had one hand covering his nose and one hand on Genie's shoulder. They walked out the doors of the cafeteria and down the hall. They stopped at the door to the nurse's office. Genie gripped the handle and pushed open the door. Nurse Wilson sat at her desk. She looked up when the two entered. She stood and stared at them.

"Well, it looks like the roles have been reversed."

She said taking Carson's hand from his nose.

"Oh, my, okay. We'll take care of you."

She sat him down on the edge of the medical bed. She got bottles of disinfectant out and a roll of medical tape. She noticed that Genie was still standing and watching.

"Thank you, Genie. You can go back to class."

Carson looked over at her. He looked like a child in so much pain. He was so mature in his usual state, now he looked so young, so innocent.

Genie looked at him warily before turning to leave. As she walked through the halls, there was not one student wandering about. Genie didn't know what to think. Was she happy that Tyler did that for her? Was she flattered? Was she mad that he hurt someone that she cared about? Did she still want to be with Carson after he stood her up? Did he still want to be with her? What was going on? As she walked through the halls, she tried to comprehend all that had happened. When she passed the office, she looked in the glass wall that stood between her and the office. Inside, Tyler sat facing the other direction. The principal's face was a bright red and his finger was wagging a few inches from Tyler's face. Addie was standing in the far corner, crying and letting all her emotions pour out in front of the office staff. Addie looked over as Genie stared in. Their eyes met and Addie's crystal eyes peered through Genie. She gasped and Addie went back to crying. Genie's thoughts dashed between Tyler and Carson. They were two completely different people and she cared for them both in very unique ways. It was like two worlds crashed together in an incredible collision. She didn't want to see Tyler get suspended but it pained her to think back to Carson on the ground. She couldn't go back to class. Not now. She didn't even know if she could handle being in the building, let alone in a class. Genie turned down a hall. She stopped in front of her locker. She removed the lock and grabbed her bag. She glanced at the sparkly ribbon, not appreciating its presence. She shut the door and walked down the hall toward one of the exits. She pushed open the doors and left the building and the drama behind her. She was the second person to successfully skip class but no one even noticed. She didn't need to get in trouble or the drama that was going on. She didn't need any of it.

Chapter 19

Genie never skipped school but today seemed like a unique circumstance. Tyler, one of her best and most trusted friends, punched the guy she was dating. She didn't know whom she was mad at. Was she angry with Carson for standing her up a few days ago? What about Tyler? He took matters into his own hands when it was none of his business. Was it flattering or out of line? Was Carson okay? Genie thought about all the questions she had as she sat on the old pier.

Her knees were tucked in tight against her chest. She was still in her uniform and her blue fleece covered her arms. The waves crashed and the water calmed her as she sat. It was freezing out but she didn't care. She couldn't go home. Not that she really wanted to anyway. The wind made her blonde hair dance around her face. She wiped a tear that dripped down her face. How could this all be happening? Was Carson okay? Was Tyler okay? How about Addie? Was Tyler pleased with what he'd done? Why?

Genie sat and watched as the turbulent waves crashed up against the wooden poles that held the old pier up from the Bay waters. The wind picked up and the cold air chilled her to the bone. Her body trembled and she couldn't help from shivering, from nerves and the cold. Tears streamed down her pale cheeks. Genie may have lived in a pretty little house with the white picket fence, but her life was far from perfect.

She missed her dad more than ever. He would have been the man that would go and talk to Carson and set him straight. Ellen would never do that. She wasn't intimidating at all and she would have no idea what to say. Dad would leave work early and come to comfort Genie when her world was falling apart. If she called her mom, Ellen would yell at Genie for disrupting her at work.

Genie felt completely alone on the pier and to a certain extent, that's just the way she wanted it. She looked down at her phone. No one had called. About two hours had passed since she first went into the lunchroom. Before any of this mess had happened. There was no one to talk to. No one would ever understand. Carson was sweet, kind, and smart. He had been her knight in shining armor. He was funny and charming and artistic. He was perfect. He had also stood her up. He let her sit in the rain, crying. He caused her pain. He let her down. Why hadn't he come? Why didn't he call?

A warm tear slid down her wind blown cheek. He stood her up. What about Tyler? He had always been there for her. He was her best friend. Well, he used to be. He'd never been violent before. He was a pacifist. He didn't like fights. Why would he belt Carson? How could he be so inconsiderate? Carson was new to the school. Tyler was making him look bad. He should have been showing him the building after school not showing him the nurse's office from the view of the table. The only reason Tyler even knew Carson existed was thanks to Genie. She had told Tyler about Carson because they were dating. Now Tyler wanted to play hero and hurt her boyfriend. How dare he! That was her business, not his. Tyler needed to mind his business and not act like he cared about her.

Now Genie was angry. She wanted Carson to know that she was mad at him for standing her up and for Tyler to know that she didn't appreciate his little . . . his little . . . act. She leaned over the water and watched as it turned. Her life seemed as complicated as all that went on in the bay waters. She could hear a car pass by on the road above. The tears had stopped but she knew it wasn't over. She'd cry again soon.

She felt a hand on her shoulder and she almost jumped out of her skin.

"Mind if I sit?" A deep voice said.

"Sure, it's a free country."

She squinted and looked at the horizon. A tear slid down her cheek even though she didn't want it to. Carson used his thumb to wipe away the tear.

"What's wrong?"

He said, his voice sounding nasal from the bandage. She sniffled before answering, "Are you okay?"

"Yeah, I'm fine. My nose isn't broken or anything," he reassured her. Genie looked at him. He had a big, white bandage across his nose and medical tape that stretched to mid-cheek.

"Oh my gosh. That looks terrible," she said covering her mouth with her hand.

"Oh sure, thanks," he laughed, "Don't worry. It doesn't hurt. It did but not anymore," he said nonchalantly.

Genie nodded and replied, "Look, I'm sorry. I didn't tell him to do that. I don't know why Tyler,"

"Don't worry. I know it wasn't your fault. You didn't hit me. I gotta tell you though; your friend can really pack a punch. Whoo."

Genie felt bad. It was her fault his nose was wrapped up.

"I think he might have done it because he picked me up and brought me home on Saturday and I was pretty upset and,"

"Yeah, I wanted to tell you about that. I didn't stand you up."

She exhaled sharply.

"Hm, well that's what it looked like."

"No," he said, "my dad came to the house. When I came back from work he was there. He was sitting at the table . . . drinking. He can get pretty bad when he drinks. My mom was terrified. He kept asking why she left and that she should come back. He kept saying he wanted his son back. I told him that there was no way in hell that I'd ever go with him. He didn't catch on. He took a swing at my mom. I, uh,"

"Oh my gosh, Carson. I'm sorry. What happened? Did he leave?"

Genie gasped in a panic. Now she felt guilty for being so angry.

"Yeah, uh, he left. He shouldn't come back anytime soon."

She reached over and wrapped her arms around his neck. She just wanted to hold him and tell him it was okay. Genie felt a chill rise from her butt through her spine. She was mad because he missed their date when he was protecting his family. He had some issues. His mom left his dad because he was cheating. His dad was a violent man who could probably hurt him. Genie couldn't imagine if his dad had hurt him. What would she do without him?

"I'm so sorry, Car. Is there anything I can do?"

He cleared his throat and looked at her. There was a tear rolling down his cheek.

"Don't leave me, 'Kay?" he begged.

His voice cracked and he sniffled. He was crying. His parents' arguing had hurt him to the point of tears. She'd never seen a guy cry other than Noah. She laid her head on his chest and replied, "Never."

Chapter 20

"So if you could please hand in your papers. Just leave them on my desk," the journalism teacher requested.

Genie sighed. She'd done hers last night at around midnight about a book she had read two years ago. There was no way she could expect anything higher than a B-. Everyone in the class stood and the bell rang. Mr. Watson was leaning against his desk watching as all his students dropped their papers in a messy pile.

"Oh, Genie, good."

She looked up and Mr. Watson was staring at her.

"I've been meaning to talk to you," he said walking around to the other side of his desk.

"Oh, okay," she said not knowing what at all this could be about.

"How is your essay coming along," he said.

"Essay? I don't know what you mean."

"The one for the University of Maryland competition. I'm very interested in reading it before you send it off."

"Oh sure, no problem. I'll bring you a copy whenever I'm done," she said sheepishly having forgotten all about the contest.

Everyone had cleared the room and she turned to leave.

"Wonderful," he said as she walked out.

That essay was due in two weeks and she'd completely forgotten about it. What was the topic again? She was so far behind and with each class, she got even more behind. This week she'd skipped half a day of classes and not even gone to school the next day. She didn't know where this behavior was coming from. She tried to explain what the situation was to her mother. Ellen didn't understand what the big deal was but mom's never understood. She had agreed to let Genie stay home because if she kept fighting, she'd never get out the door. That was Wednesday morning.

That afternoon, Genie went and saw her dad's grave. She'd been missing him a lot lately. He seemed closer than ever but not quite close enough. She walked up to the tombstone where it said, "Victor Anderson. 1959-2002. Husband, Father, Hero."

One warm tear slid down her cheek as she reread it over and over again. He was a hero. He'd been a hero to so many people and now he wasn't there anymore and the world seemed to be fine. After there were no more tears to cry, Genie sat with her back against a tree and talked to the grave. She talked for hours. She talked about Carson, Tyler, Trinity, Mom, Noah, Poppy, school, the weather, what's been on T.V, the gazette, and anything she could think about. It was just like old times. She'd talk and dad listened.

The flowers she brought were blue hydrangeas. He never liked pink flowers, so no one ever brought him a feminine colored flower. When a car passed by, Genie realized how long she'd been there.

"Sorry, dad, I gotta go. I'll talk to you later. Bye."

She got up to leave. When she got to her car, she turned around and waved. Even though there was no one there, Dad seemed to wave back.

"Hey," Carson said stepping in front of her.

He had gotten the bandage taken off from when Tyler had punched him. He had a scar on his nose. It was small but if you knew where to look, it wasn't that hard to find.

"Well, hello there. Fancy meeting you here," she giggled.

"I think I've heard that somewhere before."

Carson stroked his chin and looked off into the distance as if he was thinking about something.

"Sorry if I sound rude but what do you need? I'm gonna be late for class," she said turning and grabbing a few books from her locker.

"Oh, okay. I'll make it speedy," He said taking a deep breath. "I was wondering if you wanted to come to this dance with me. I heard it'll be cheesy boring and cliche everything I ever wanted, Please?"

He said it so fast that she had barely heard every word.

"Sure," she laughed.

"Great. I'll pick you up tomorrow at say, six?" He said relieved.

"Sounds good. Am I expected to wear a dress or is it casual?"

"I don't know about you," he said, "but I'm planning to wear a classy cocktail dress." She laughed.

"Alright, dress it is."

"Great," he said.

He leaned over and gave her a quick peck on the lips.

"I'll see you later."

"Okay, wait I have a question," she said.

"Yeah?"

"Where did you learn to be so charming?" she sarcastically asked.

He laughed and rubbed the back of his neck, "I watch a lot of T.V."

She laughed. How could she say no to going to a dance with him? She had always hated dances because they were long, boring, and cliché. All the popular girls, like Lindsey, got expensive dresses and went to the salon to get their hair done. They danced with their boyfriends all night long and all the dorks and nerds stood in the corner and watched, wondering if they were even capable of having a good time. Genie was somewhere in the middle. She danced to a few songs with some friends and then hung around the punch bowl and talked to other people the rest of the time.

It wouldn't be that bad now that she had Carson. Knowing him, they'd be on the dance floor all night.

She walked to her next class, which just happened to be a study hall. There were a few paintings hanging in the hall. One of them was of a pier and a girl sitting with her legs dangling off. Genie looked down to the bottom.

"Serenity, by Carson Knight."

Her heart sped up. Was that her? She didn't have time to look at it now. She opened the door and walked in. Addie was sitting next to some girl with glasses. When Genie walked in, Addie looked up and went back to working. What was with the attitude? When she looked around the classroom, Genie noticed that Tyler wasn't there. Had he gotten suspended? Expelled? Genie tried not to think the worst. She sat down at a table by herself and thought about what she'd wear to the dance tomorrow. She didn't have any dresses that she hadn't worn before. Crap! Ellen would definitely not be up for shopping tonight. What was she going to wear? She didn't have any money. She tried to think if anyone she knew would let her borrow one. Addie might have one. She looked over and noticed that the girl that had been sitting next to Addie had gone to the bathroom. Genie moved over and sat next to her.

"Hey," Genie said.

"What do you want," she replied.

"I was wondering if you had a dress I could borrow. Carson's taking me to that dance tomorrow and I'm out of dresses."

"Sorry, I don't."

"Okay . . ." Genie said, beginning to feel the tension.

Addie got up and the chair she was sitting in flew back. She stormed across the room, opened the door and let it slam behind her. The teacher watched Addie then turned to Genie. Addie had never been mad at her before. What was she mad about? Genie stared at the floor than walked back to her seat. Why did everything have to be so dramatic? This wasn't a soap opera. Their ratings weren't dropping. This was just every day life and no one cared about Addie's little drama. Genie went back to working. She didn't want to think about Addie when there were History questions calling her name.

"Mom, is that you?" Noah called from his room.

Genie lay on her bed, staring at the ceiling.

"Yeah, its me." Ellen was just getting back from work.

She sounded like she was in a good mood, which meant she might be willing to help her daughter find a dress. Genie had lay on her bed with a notebook for an hour. She kept running over different things that she had experienced in her life but she couldn't think of one question that she could answer that would win the Maryland Writing Competition. Nothing she thought of was interesting. She could hear footsteps coming up the stairs.

"Noah, you're backpack is downstairs, unzipped. I want you to go and do your homework. Now."

Noah groaned and he walked to where Ellen was standing at the top of the staircase.

"Hey, mom," Genie said flipping onto her stomach.

"Yes, Genesis."

Ellen stood in the doorframe of the room. She had her hands on her hips but she didn't look impatient or angry.

"Carson's taking me to that dance tomorrow and I don't have a dress."

"I thought you broke up with him?" her mother quizzed.

Genie's heart dropped. Something about the thought of breaking up with Carson made her extremely sad, lonely, and scared at the same time.

"No, it was a big misunderstanding. So do you know of any dresses?" Genie said trying to quickly change the subject.

"Well," Ellen said walking in.

"I think you have some really nice ones in here."

She was sifting through the things hanging up in her closet.

"I've worn all of those already and I wanna look really nice," Genie begged.

Ellen turned around with a black dress in her hand. It was knee length and it had thick straps. It was very plain and simple.

"Ew," Genie said, "it looks like I'd wear that to a funeral. Yuck! Too depressing." Ellen put it back and stared at her daughter on the bed.

"You really like this boy don't you?"

Genie could feel the heat rise to her cheeks.

"Yeah, I do."

"OK, well then, follow me."

Ellen sauntered out of the room. Genie quickly rose and followed her as she walked down the hall. She made a left into Trinity's room. Ellen reached into the closet. Genie plopped down on the bed. Nothing about Trinity's room had changed since she had left in the fall. It looked like she still lived there. There were crumpled up pieces of paper that still hadn't managed to make it into the trashcan and clothes that hadn't made it to the hamper. Trinity's room was a pale pink and her bedspread was pink and brown striped. Ellen pulled out a teal dress with white detailing. It was gorgeous.

"Mom, it's so pretty." Genie gushed.

Ellen eyed it over and smiled.

"Trinity said she hated it when I bought it for her."

"That's probably why I like it." They both laughed.

"Try it on. I wanna see what it looks like," Ellen requested.

Genie took the dress and slipped it on. She looked in Trinity's mirror. It fit perfectly. Genie smiled and turned to her mother who was now sitting on the bed.

"Oh my gosh, its perfect."

Genie turned back to the mirror to see it again.

"Hey, Genesis?"

"Yeah, mom."

"Could I help you get ready tomorrow? I've never helped you get ready for a dance before and I'd really like to."

Ellen sounded so meek and insecure. She had never asked to help Genie with anything. She never seemed to care before.

"Yeah, mom, of course."

Genie unzipped the dress and put her pajama pants back on.

"Oh, great."

Ellen's face lit up as she turned to leave.

"Mom."

Genie surprised herself with how meekly the word came out. Ellen turned around. "Yes, dear?"

"I love you, mom."

"I love you, too, Genesis."

School was taking forever today. The cheerleaders were prancing around in their uniforms telling people to go to the dance. It actually made Genie not want to go to the dance. She rolled her eyes when Lindsey led the girls in a cheer that went something like,

"1 . . . 2 . . . 3 . . . Come to the dance and have some fun, support the school and raise some funds! Whooo!"

A monkey could have come up with that cheer.

Genie stared down at her feet and walked to her last class that day, Art. She could tell that it was going to be the first class today that would fly by. Things hadn't been too great at school because the only person she was talking to was Carson.

Addie was acting weird and so was Tyler. She didn't need them anyway.

She walked into the classroom and sat down on a stool. There were fifteen stools and easels set up around the room. They all were set up so that when a student sat down, they faced the middle of the room. In the middle was the art teacher, Ms. Jamison. Genie watched as Ms. Jamison walked around the room handing out scraps of cloth.

"What we're going to learn about now is art involving fabric. Usually, when we paint, we use paper but art stretches to all kinds of materials. Please take your fabric and paint a scene that calms you or brings you happiness," instructed Mr. Jamison.

Genie stared at the white cloth that was pinned to her easel. She thought about what she found calming. She thought about music, her backyard, her house, then, she had it. She began to paint. She eyed over the cloth. Her hand made swift movements over the easel. She dipped her brush in a jar of blue paint. She pressed the brush on cloth and she painted. She didn't even notice the time passing as she painted. Ms. Jamison sauntered over to where Genie sat.

"Well, that's just beautiful. Good job," Ms. Jamison said eyeing the piece.

"I never knew you were talented at art," Ms. Jamison continued to gush enthusiastically.

Genie was stunned at her comment.

"Yeah," she said, "Me neither."

Ms. Jamison winked at her and pointed to the water in the painting.

"There's a heart in the water."

Ms. Jamison surveyed the cloth. She had painted the pier and the water.

Sitting at the pier calmed her. On the cloth was the brown pier, it sat centered and water seemed to move in waves at the bottom. The upper half was painted a light gray, almost blue. There were a few clouds scattered throughout what was the sky. One of the clouds was shaped like a cross. It was just like what Carson had painted but she put her heart in it.

"Yeah, I thought the heart in the waves was a nice touch," Genie replied.

Ms. Jamison nodded and walked on. Genie had never been good at art. She had never tried. She stared at the painted cloth, and for the first time ever, she was proud of something she had made. She liked it. Mason walked by and stopped.

"Oh, cool." he commented.

His sparkling brown eyes assessed the painting and then Genie. She rolled her eyes. She had poured her heart onto a cloth and through a painting and all he said was 'cool'? She now understood why things never went anywhere between her and Mason, and she was glad. He walked away and went to some other girl's painting. He was a player and she was glad she was with Carson and not that loser. She absolutely loved the painting and who cares what anyone else thought?

Chapter 21

"So how do you want your hair, straight or curly?" Ellen said standing over her daughter.

"Curly, I guess." Genie replied.

"OK, I'll curl it for you."

Genie sat and thought about Carson as her mom wove the hot curling iron through her blonde hair.

"So tell me about this Carson boy. I don't really know him."

Ellen started her questioning. Genie sighed.

"Well, he's an artist. He's really good too. He can paint just about anything, including people," her mind drifted to the painting in the hallway.

"Oh that's nice." Ellen said condescendingly.

"Yea, he plays hockey too. He used to live in D.C." Genie continued explaining.

"Oh, really. That's interesting. What do his parents do?"

Genie's mind clouded with Carson's stories about his father and mother.

"His mother works somewhere around here. I forgot where. His dad isn't around. They're divorced."

"I'd love to meet his mother."

Ellen said, genuinely interested in Carson's family.

"Me too," Genie said staring at her own reflection.

"So what else should I know about Carson?"

"Um, he's very protective. He's definitely a momma's boy. Ha-ha. He's really funny. Oh, and he comes up with the most creative dates."

Ellen laughed and looked over Genie's shoulder.

"A school dance doesn't seem all that original to me."

Genie laughed.

"Well, they're usually kinda out there."

She leaned over and flipped some music on. One of the songs that had been playing at the ice rink was on.

"How did you know you loved Dad?"

Ellen sighed.

"Well, its funny you should ask. I asked my mother the same question when I met your father," Ellen reminisced.

"That's kinda weird," Genie suggested.

"I'm going to tell you what she told me. It's when you love them for their nice qualities and their faults. You love it when they chew like a cow and embarrass you in restaurants. You love them even when they'd rather sit and watch the football game instead of helping fold laundry. She said that you love someone when you cannot imagine your world without them."

Ellen sniffled a little. Genie looked up and noticed a tear streaming down Ellen's face. "Mom, what's wrong?"

Ellen looked Genie in the eyes and said, "I couldn't imagine my world without your father but I had to learn how."

Genie smiled. It was a bittersweet feeling.

"Hello, Mrs. Anderson."

"Hello, Carson. Please come in."

"Thank you."

Carson stepped inside the house.

"Would you like anything to drink?"

Ellen asked walking into the kitchen. Carson took a seat on the sofa and looked at the family portrait hanging above the mantel. They looked like a perfect family.

"Carson, its nice to get to talk to you in a calm setting. I was a little stressed in the hospital. I've heard so much about you."

Carson grinned.

"Good things, I hope."

Ellen poked her head in from the kitchen.

"Better than you can imagine."

He smiled. His suit was kind of uncomfortable. He felt like one of those cheesy guys from a teen movie. It's the kind of movie where the girl struts down from the stairs and he can't breathe. Than they all live happily ever after. It was all very cliché.

Ellen called, "Genesis, Carson is here."

He chuckled. Genesis. Who picks a name like that?

He could hear the footsteps and he rose. He walked over to the bottom of the staircase and waited for Genie to come, as he assumed he was required to do. She turned the corner and began to walk down the stairs. She was stunning. Her blue-ish green dress had white flowers stitched on. Her hair was pulled back halfway and it was curled like on their first date. She was wearing a cross necklace and white heels. He'd never seen her so beautiful. She smiled, revealing her perfectly white teeth. When she reached the bottom of the steps, he cleared his throat.

"You look really pretty," he offered. He was so awkward.

Genie smiled and looped her arm through his.

"Aw, so do you," she said.

Ellen came from the kitchen with a camera. She had one of the old ones.

"Just one picture," Genie cautioned.

The flash went off and the picture slid from the camera. Genie didn't bother to see how it turned out. She was already leading him out the door.

"It was nice seeing you, Mrs. Anderson," Carson called into the house as he was being dragged away.

"Nice seeing you again," Ellen called out in reply.

Genie stared at Carson as he danced beside her. The DJ was playing another upbeat song and everyone hit the dance floor. The night had been going fairly well. Genie introduced Carson to a couple people that she had classes with and talked to. He had been kind and very friendly. He introduced her to a few of his friends. One named Scott who was with a girl named Samantha and another guy named Anthony who didn't have a date with him. His friends seemed a lot more immature but they seemed to be relatively polite.

The popular cheerleaders and football players danced together. Half of them had been drinking, you could tell. Lindsey had her arms around Mason.

A month or two ago, she would have been jealous and angry. Now she was glad because she had a real man of her own. Her man looked quite snazzy. Carson was wearing a black suit and blue shirt. He looked very awkward in the suit. He was definitely a denim and flannel kind of guy.

The decorations were cheesy. It was an ocean theme and there were blue and green balloons. There were mermaid paintings and the teachers were dressed up as sailors. It was all a little ridiculous. The DJ screamed in the microphone, "All right ladies and gents, we're gonna slow things down a little bit."

Then a sappy slow song came on and everyone in the room immediately coupled up. Carson turned to Genie. She put her arms around his neck and he grabbed her waist. He smelled nice.

"So, things exciting enough for you?" he asked her.

She laughed at his question.

"I'm on edge," she replied sarcastically.

They were so close that their noses almost touched. He breathed a deep breath and leaned over to whisper in her ear, "I want you to meet someone tonight."

"Okay," she said.

She leaned her head on his shoulder. There were about 120 other people in the school gym but it felt like they were alone. When the song stopped, Carson took her hand and pulled.

"Where are you going?" she questioned.

He turned back.

"Come with me."

Genie followed him out of the gym and to his car. The pavement was wet and the air was damp. No one was in the parking lot except for them. He was still holding her hand when they got to his car. He quickly grabbed her and kissed her right there. When he pulled back, she looked at him.

"I have to say, Carson Knight, you choose the most interesting places to kiss me." She said in the softest voice she had ever used.

He smiled and hugged her.

"I thought lips were fine."

She laughed and went around to the passenger seat. It was turning out to be the perfect night. Genie looked out the passenger seat window as they pulled up to a small house. It was a single-family house that didn't have much of a yard. It was a light gray and it had two windows on the front side. It was a small house but it looked really cozy.

"Well, this is my house," Carson said as he was getting out of the car and opening the door for her.

"Thanks," she said as she stepped out.

He walked up the driveway and to the front door.

"Am I going to finally meet your mother?" she questioned excitedly.

Carson nodded. He opened the door and the smell of fresh baked bread overwhelmed Genie as she stepped in. The living room was white and had some blue furniture. The kitchen was straight ahead, just like in her own house.

"Mom, there's someone I'd like you to meet," Carson announced.

A brunette holding a plastic bowl turned from the stove.

"Oh, my goodness! You must be Genie!" the brunette gushed.

Genie felt herself blushing.

The woman rushed over and stuck out her hand. There was dough on her hands and flour in her hair and on her face.

"Oh, I'm sorry. I'll be right back," she said excusing herself.

She rushed down a hallway and when she came back, she had taken off her apron and had washed her face and hands.

Carson looked at Genie and smiled.

"Mom, this is Genesis Anderson. Genie, this is my mother."

Genie stuck out her hand but Carson's mom reached over and hugged

"It's nice to meet you, Ms. Knight."

Genie said, taken back by the hug.

"Oh, please. My name's Veronica. Call me that. Do either of you want something to eat or drink?"

Carson was sitting on the sofa, so Genie joined him.

"No thank you," she said.

Carson replied, "Hey mom, can you bring me a Coke?"

"Yeah, alright."

She came back in with three cans.

"Genesis, we're big drinkers in this house so I'm gonna force you to take one."

Genie smiled. Carson leaned in to her, "She means Coke. We drink a lot of soda."

"So Genesis," Veronica said sitting in an armchair across from the sofa,

"How do you spell your name?"

"Well, actually, I go by Genie. It's G-E-N-I-E."

Veronica nodded.

"I'd think that sounded like Jeanne. But you say it like Jenny."

"I don't know. I've always spelled it that way."

Veronica took a sip from the soda can.

"So Carson tells me you are quite the writer."

Genie looked over at him. He was blushing and staring at the floor.

"Well, I love to write," Genie said.

Veronica continued, "I've never been very good at writing. It's a wonder I passed my English classes. Carson and I have always been artists."

Genie looked around the room suddenly noticing all the paintings. There were six in this room and more around the house. There was one of a city at night. There were two of a young boy, not Carson, but someone who looked like him. Veronica noticed Genie staring at one of a young boy with a baseball bat and hat.

"If you're wondering, that's Landon. He's my other son. He's 14. Him and Jeff used to go and play baseball together whenever they got the chance."

Carson cleared his throat.

"But that's all in the past," Veronica said looking down at her torn jeans. For the first time, Genie noticed there was a large bruise on Carson's mom's arm. It wasn't the type of bruise you got from falling off a chair. Someone had hit or grabbed her.

"Genie has a younger brother too," Carson said breaking the unbearable silence.

"Oh, yeah?" Veronica said perking up.

"How old?"

"Ten. He's a good kid," Genie said.

Carson added, "Yeah, he's doing the pine box derby thing up on Main Street tomorrow."

"Ah, neat. I saw some posters about that. Good for him," Veronica encouraged.

Genie liked Veronica. She was nothing like Ellen. Veronica was creative, unique, positive, and funny. Ellen was simple, boring, and a by-the-book type of mother. Genie saw why Carson was so unique and kind. The apple didn't fall far from the tree.

Veronica looked down at her mini mouse watch.

"It's almost eleven. I don't know about your mother but I'd want my daughter home soon," she said with concern.

"Hey, you don't care about your son?" Carson joked.

"Well, you're different, Car," she said waving his complaint off.

Carson stood and so did Genie. Veronica stood in the doorway as Genie got into Carson's car. She waved good-bye and Genie waved back. Carson started the car.

"Your mom is really nice," she said buckling her seat belt.

"Yeah, she likes you."

Genie looked at him surprised.

"She does? She didn't say anything."

"I could tell," he said.

Genie stared at him as he watched the road. He seemed older than his age. His parents' messy divorce had aged him and he'd never get the years back. His short dirty blonde hair and dark greenish-gray eyes looked serious. He looked over at her.

"What?" he questioned.

"Nothing," she said, "Just looking."

He pulled up to her house and stopped. She looked at him and he at her.

They shared a long kiss before she stepped out of the car.

"Hey, lets do something tomorrow," he said breaking the silence.

"Okay, what time will you pick me up?" she asked.

He looked outside his window and replied, "How about ten. Is that too early? Brunch maybe?"

"Alright," she smiled.

"That sounds lame?" He asked.

"A tiny bit," she laughed, "It's a good thing you're cute."

"I do try," he laughed.

"Bye," he kissed her again.

She shut the door behind her and ran to the house. Her heels clicked and clacked all the way up to her room. She plopped down on her bed and her head swirled with emotion. She was so happy that she had him. They always had a good time. She was also sad because he didn't have a dad in his life just like her. But that only made them closer. She rolled over and fell asleep in her dress and heels. She used to always wish to be asleep and dreaming but now, when she was awake and with Carson, it was better than any dream.

Chapter 22

The doorbell rang and Genie's eyes flipped open. She could hear people moving around downstairs. It wasn't the usual Saturday morning sluggish movements. It was chaotic movements. Genie peeked downstairs and when she saw Ellen rushing around with a cooler, she thought better and went back to her room.

"Noah, let's go! You don't wanna be late."

Ellen was stressed. Anyone could have seen that.

"Okay. One sec, I'm just putting on my lucky underwear," Noah replied.

Ew, gross! Noah never had a good sense of what was public and private information.

A deep voice laughed, "Alright, well you aren't going to need luck today. We built a great racer. You're gonna fly past everyone else."

Tyler? Genie went back and looked downstairs. Tyler was standing at the bottom of the steps and when he saw Genie, they both jumped.

"Sorry, Genie. I didn't see you there," he offered quickly, almost shyly.

She was still a little asleep so it took her a minute to respond.

"Yeah, me neither."

She blinked and realized she was still wearing Trinity's dress and her hair was a mess. He was chewing gum but the squishy, sloppy sound made her feel sick. She had never been a morning person and she could feel her own attitude pinching her nerves.

"Is that what you're wearing? Better get changed, we're all leaving soon," Tyler questioned.

"What time is it?" She asked groggily.

Boy, that gum sound was irritating. She could smell the citrus scent from the top of the stairs.

He flipped open his cell phone and replied, "9:22. Noah, hurry up!"

"Alright!"

Noah's little voice sounded mute compared to the rushing around downstairs.

"Hey, Genie, who are you gonna ride with up there?" Ellen asked up the stairs.

"Up where?" Genie was so dazed with all of the confusion. Tyler looked stunned.

"To the derby?" Ellen said with an accusing look.

Genie's heart dropped. Noah's race was today. She hadn't even thought about it.

"Uh, I'm not gonna make it on time. I'll try and be there at the end though."

Tyler looked offended.

"What do you mean you're not going to make it?" He asked as accusingly as Ellen looked.

Genie put one hand on her hip.

"You heard me. I can't go right now. Also, that gum is way too disgusting at this time of the morning."

Tyler turned his head and looked back at her. He stuck his hand in his mouth and pulled the gum out with an attitude. When he turned back, his eyes were wild with rage.

"It's Carson isn't it?" He said angrily trying not to spit.

"Maybe it is. Is that a problem for you?" Genie replied equally as angrily.

Tyler was tapping his foot impatiently.

"You're gonna miss your brother's race because of some guy?!" Tyler's rant continued.

"He's not just some guy!"

She raised her voice.

Tyler quickly snapped, "You're right! Noah's not just some guy either. He's your brother!"

"You don't even know Carson! All you know is that he's got a nose that you almost broke!" she countered.

Tyler turned his head like he'd just been slapped across the cheek.

"Whatever, I don't care."

"I don't care either! Go to the stupid race! Good luck!"

Genie whipped around and turned to her room. She slammed the door.

Tyler screamed, "Noah! Now!"

He didn't sound impatient at all. It was pure anger. She could hear Noah running down the stairs. There were voices downstairs but she couldn't make out what they were saying. Then the front door closed and it was quiet. She looked at her alarm clock. It was 9:30. Carson would be here in a half an hour. She quickly jumped in the shower. She thought about what Tyler had said. Who did he think he was? He was telling her what to do. Well it wasn't any of his business. He's just jealous because he doesn't have anyone. He couldn't even hold onto that tramp, Lindsey.

Noah didn't care if she went. It wasn't like he was going to win. She changed into a pair of denim shorts and a sweater. Her hair was still wet and wrapped in a towel on the top of her head. She had no makeup on and she had dark circles under her eyes. She looked terrible. The doorbell rang and she skipped downstairs.

Carson was standing at the door with a bouquet of flowers.

Genie eyed them, "For me?"

He looked in the house suspiciously.

"Actually, I was going to give these to your mom."

"My mom?"

Genie questioned. Carson set them down on the table.

"Not like that. I'm always taking her daughter away from her so I felt kinda bad. I brought flowers."

"Oh, okay. That's not weird at all. Here, I'll put them in some water."

She picked up the flowers and went into the kitchen. Carson sat down on the sofa.

"Where is everyone?"

Genie yelled from the kitchen, "They're at Noah's thing."

"Oh, shit, do you wanna go to that. I'll drive," Carson apologized.

Genie walked in and sat next to him, "Nope. I wanna stay here."

He kissed her and smiled.

"Oh, there's something I want to show you," she pulled him down the steps and out the back door. In the backyard there was a small garden and a plaque. Blue Hydrangeas surrounded the plaque and it said:

"Victor, we'll always love you. Be with us."

Carson smiled. He looked at Genie who was still staring at the plaque.

She looked at him and thought about what her mother had said.

You know you love someone when you can't imagine your life without them.

"I love you," she said.

He looked into her eyes. Her heart stopped. What if he didn't love her? What if she wasn't supposed to say it?

"I love you, too."

Her heart melted and she knew he meant it. He leaned over and kissed her. At first it was soft then a little harder. She held his neck and he grabbed her waist. She pulled back and ran back into the house and up to her room.

She sat on her bed and he came running after her. He wrapped his arms around her and they were making out a few minutes when he reached for her shirt before Genie stopped him.

"What?" He asked leaning back.

"I don't wanna go any farther," she said.

She wasn't ready and she knew it. Her mom had talked to her when she was a little younger and she knew all about the dangers that came with sex and she wasn't ready.

He exhaled. "Are you sure?"

What kind of question was that?

She thought but said, "Uh, yeah, I'm pretty sure."

He plopped down on the bed on his back and stared at the ceiling.

"What are you waiting for?" he asked impatiently.

She could feel her face get hot.

"I don't know but I haven't waited this long to mess it all up now," she said.

"So you think I'm messing things up?" he asked dejectedly.

"No, not at all. I just want to wait."

She tried to sooth his ego. He sighed and looked at her. She stared back at him. He leaned towards her and hugged her.

"Okay, I guess I should understand, huh?" he said.

"Well," she said, "I think it'd be kinda weird if . . . and then I went to church. God's not a huge fan. He likes people to wait."

He nodded.

"Alright, fine."

She chuckled and he hugged her.

He kissed the top of her forehead. Maybe he would understand eventually. He was a guy after all. It might take a while. They went down stairs and watched a movie. Just as the movie was ending, the phone rang. Genie got up and answered.

Chapter 23

"Hello?"

"Hi, Genesis."

It was Ellen.

"Hey, mom. What's up?"

"Are you sitting down?" Ellen asked.

"Yeah," Genie lied.

The nearest chair was a few feet away and she didn't feel like getting it.

"Honey, Tyler was in an accident . . ."

Thump.

Carson heard a loud bang and jumped up. He ran to the kitchen and on the tile floor, Genie was laying. The phone was hanging on the chord.

He picked up the phone, "Hello?"

"Carson, it's Mrs. Anderson. What . . . Where's Genesis?"

Ellen sounded panicked and in the background, Carson could hear a police car or ambulance. "I think . . . I think she fainted. What's going on? What's wrong?"

Ellen was weeping on the other side of the line.

"Tyler's on his way to the hospital. He was in a bad accident," she sobbed.

"Oh my God," he said.

She continued, "He was driving back from the race and a truck made a sharp turn. He swerved to not get hit and he went over the guardrail and into the water."

Carson looked at Genie's body lying on the floor.

"Mrs. Anderson, I gotta get Genie and uh, I'll meet you at the, uh, hospital."

He hung up the phone and knelt beside Genie. She was breathing but she was out cold. He went to the sink and took of his T-shirt. He wet the shirt and dabbed cold water on her face. She opened her eyes. He leaned back and took a deep breath. She was back.

"What's going on?" she asked

How could he be the one to remind her that Tyler was hurt?

"We gotta go to the hospital."

It was all he could think to say.

Genie ran through the automatic doors to the hospital. Ellen and Noah were sitting on chairs in the waiting room. There were about fifteen other people in the waiting room but no one else that she recognized. There was an African American nurse in white, standing in the corner, watching. Genie turned to her family and looked from her mom to her brother.

"What's going on?" She asked frantically.

Her heart was racing and she couldn't catch her breath. Carson walked in and approached where she was standing.

Ellen looked at Carson then back to Genie, "Genesis, sweetheart, Tyler was in a very bad accident. The doctors just came out and told us about what's going on."

"Well?" She asked as Ellen wiped a tear from her eye.

She cried gracefully, not in a panicked or in an uncontrollable way. She simply had a tear running down her cheek.

"Tyler suffered severe head trauma and some broken ribs. He broke something in his spine. I can't remember the exact term. He has fluid in his lungs and there is a very good chance that he's not going to make it," Ellen tried to explain.

Noah let out a scream and he doubled over. He started bawling and his little body shook in the big plastic chair. Genie looked at him and then back at Ellen. Ellen was crying too, wiping her tears with a tissue. Carson was running his hand through his hair. Genie looked around the waiting room. No one else she knew was there. Why wasn't anyone here? Where was everyone? Did they not want to come? Did they not care?

"Well, he's gonna live. I know he will. It's Tyler."

Genie tried explaining all of Tyler's injuries away.

Ellen looked at her shoes as she continued, "If he does make it, he will have lost his entire memory and he'll have to relearn everything. He won't know how to walk, read, or write. If he lives, he'll be like an infant."

Genie could feel her stomach flip.

"What do you mean 'if'? He's gonna make it, mom! You don't understand!"

Ellen's facial muscles went tense. She was stricken with pain as she tried to speak softly to her daughter, "Calm down."

Genie's voice rose, "Where are the Moore's?"

Ellen looked to a pair of double doors. The same nurse in white was staring at them. She looked a little creepy but Genie didn't notice.

"They are talking with some doctors to find out if they can see him before he dies," Ellen said.

"I wanna see him!" Genie said standing, "I have to!"

She suddenly felt very dizzy and out of control. She stuck her arms out for balance but it didn't help. Carson grabbed her arm to steady her. Ellen reached out but didn't touch her. She jerked away and ran to the double doors.

Where is he? There were three hallways and she had no idea which way to go. It looked like a maze. A nurse stopped her and asked where she was going.

"I gotta see him," she replied.

She made it another few feet before she was faced with two more hallways. She leaned against the wall and slid down. She wept and as people passed her, they stared, but she didn't care. The colors of the hospital seemed to blur together and no one seemed to look real. Nothing seemed real. She lay on the floor and cried until a nurse came to her.

"Honey, what are you doing?"

The nurse was wearing cream, almost white scrubs that had little angels on them. She had dark skin and black hair. Her hair was in small braids. She was heavier set and was carrying a clipboard. She knelt beside Genie and stroked her back.

"There, there," she tried comforting Genie.

Genie burst into another set of tears.

"Now what seems to be the problem?"

Genie looked at her. She was the same nurse that had been in the waiting room. The nurse's eyes were calm and understanding.

"I need to see him."

"See who, sweet child?" the nurse's smooth, calming voice asked.

Genie willed herself to be able to say the words. There was this enormous lump in her throat and it was hard to talk.

"Ty . . . Tyler . . . Moore."

The nurse looked down at her rubber shoes and then back at Genie. This whole thing seemed surreal. Maybe it wasn't happening.

The nurse sighed. She looked like an angel among a sea of sterile needles and bad news.

"I'm sorry, dear, he isn't here. He's passed."

Carson ran in the double doors after Genie. This was all a little crazy.

Tyler was in an accident less than an hour ago and now he's on his deathbed? Did it really happen that quickly? There were three hallways.

He turned left and kept running. He bumped into cart full of food and a nurse was yelling at him. Another two hallways confronted him. He looked ahead and saw Genie laying on the ground with an older nurse hovering over her.

"What's wrong?" He asked.

The nurse looked at him, and then back down at her. Genie looked up. There was something in her eyes that wasn't right. She wasn't hurt. She wasn't scared.

She didn't seem angry. It seemed as though she was remembering something and acting it out as she had before.

She finally spoke, "I didn't hate him. I wasn't mad. I didn't mean to yell at him. He was trying to be nice."

She sounded delirious. The nurse shook her head. It suddenly clicked. Carson stepped back.

"He's gone?"

The nurse nodded.

Genie looked up and her eyes were a different green. They were usually a calm, grass green. Now they were a stunning and sharp green that was beautiful and eerie. Her face was red and her hair was messy. She burst into tears once again. He knelt down beside her and held her. The nurse looked over the two and shook her head. She left them as quickly as she came. Carson held her as she shook. She was going out of her mind.

Doctors and nurses went by. Patients in wheelchairs passed. Nurses passed. Everyone and everything seemed to pass them, except time. Time stood still. It was all slow motion. Genie's jerking motions, slow. The tears, slow. The thoughts, slow. They lay on the floor together in the hospital for what seemed like forever.

Chapter 24

"Genesis, come down and eat."

Ellen called up to her daughter. Genie hadn't left the house in four days. She wasn't taking Tyler's death well. She was barely eating anything and she'd cried so much that she got sick a few nights ago. The funeral was tomorrow. The last time she had been outside was on Sunday evening for a candle vigil. Everyone at Blakeridge and St. Bernadette's had gathered outside the school and held candles in memory of Tyler. Some people had made posters that said things like, "We'll always miss you," and "We love you, Tyler."

Addie did not attend the service and neither did Mr. Moore. Mrs. Moore made an appearance. There was a crowd of over 900 people and as Mrs. Moore stood at the steps of the school building, she eyed the crowd and was given a megaphone.

She looked over everyone and said, "Thank you all for coming out. Thank you for your support. We all need each other's support to get through this. My boy was an amazing individual and it seems wrong that he was an angel that was taken from us all too soon. We cannot change his death but we can inspire each other's future. Please pray for my pride and joy and our family. Thank you again."

Though it was dark, that was the brightest night Genie had ever seen. Flames flickered in the hands of each person that stood in memory of Tyler. Genie stood in the front of the pack and turned to see how many had gathered. What she saw was a sea of angels. The lights lit up every face and every tear. Some people prayed while others sang. Some swayed with closed eyes and some just stared blankly ahead. It was one of the saddest times in Genie's life but it was also the most beautiful.

Everyone in the crowd lowered their head for a moment of silence but in the night air, you could hear sniffles and people crying. Genie hadn't cried at the service because she had cried all day and there were no more tears.

There were enlarged pictures of Tyler hanging from some of the windows of the school. In one of the pictures, Addie, Tyler, and Genie were standing in their uniforms outside the school building making stupid funny faces. Tyler's tongue was sticking out, Genie's eyes were crossed, and Addie was making a pig face. When Genie saw the picture-banners she smiled and thought back to when the yearbook had asked them to pose. They had thought it was hilarious at the time but now, nothing seemed funny anymore. There were other of pictures of Tyler all over the place and it only made it harder to keep everything in her mind collected. Each person in the crowd held a candle and the choir led a song and the crowd sang together the lyrics to "Lean on Me";

Sometimes in our lives we all have pain We all have sorrow But if we are wise We know that there's always tomorrow Lean on me, when you're not strong And I'll be your friend

I'll help you carry on

Genie immediately cried after hearing the lyrics. Tyler had always been there for her. If something like this had happened to someone else, Tyler would have been there. She could have leaned on him. He wasn't there anymore. She couldn't lean on him. She wouldn't be able to lean on him ever again. He was gone.

Lindsey had wailed like a baby at the service. She caused a huge scene and half the cheerleading squad had to comfort her so she could control her volume. She had treated him like dirt and now she was sorry? She chose now to be remorseful? What a bitch. Wait, but isn't that what Genie had done?

There was no one that understood the way she felt. No one else was close with him like she was. They had been best friends, up until the end, at least. What was wrong with her? Why didn't she just go to Noah's race? Maybe he wouldn't have died if she would've made him wait a minute longer, a second longer. Why did she have to yell at him before they left? Why couldn't she be polite and kind?

The guilt weighed her down like a thousand bricks. She had been so selfish. It felt like she was wasting away and that life would never be the same.

"Genesis, come down here now!"

Ellen was being forceful about her eating. Sure, she hadn't eaten much in the past few days but what did it matter? It wouldn't kill her. And if it did, who cares?

Her phone rang again. She stared at the screen. Incoming call: Carson Knight. She didn't want to talk to him. He'd been calling a lot in the past couple days. Why did he want to talk to her so badly? She didn't want to talk to him. She didn't want to talk to anyone. She let it keep ringing until it went to voicemail.

"Now!"

"FINE!"

Genie slammed the door to her bedroom and stomped down the stairs. Ellen was standing over a skillet. Ellen had taken the week off to stay with Genie and let her grieve. She didn't mention the school she was missing or the work that she'd have to make up. Ellen let Genie deal with Tyler's death as she wished. Genie stormed into the kitchen.

"I'm here, let's eat," Genie snarled.

She had been a little emotional lately. One minute she was crying. The next minute she was angry and throwing things around the house. Ellen had told her that there was no right way to grieve. Did that mean that every way was wrong? Ellen put a plate of eggs and bacon in front of Genie. A tear slid down her cheek. She picked up a fork but her hand felt so weak that it shook in her hand. She stabbed a piece of egg and brought it to her face but dropped the fork. She stood and the chair behind her slid back and fell. Ellen looked over. Genie turned and ran. She ran out of the house and to the backyard. She lay on the ground next to the hydrangeas and the plaque.

Between sobs, she cried out, "Dad, I need you! I need you! Please come home!"

Ellen watched from the window, a single tear sliding down her cheek. Genie beat her fist against the grass and cried out,

"Dad, please!"

Why wasn't he coming home? Victor had always been there. He wasn't there. He'd never be there. Now she'd lost the two most important men in her life. What had she done to deserve this? Was it because of Carson? She'd break up with him. She just wanted her dad and best friend back. It wasn't fair. Some people go through their entire lives without losing someone close to them. She lost two people in a few years. It wasn't fair! She bawled and beat the ground. The grass was cold and the air was warmer. Each blade tickled her arms but she wouldn't laugh. She'd never laugh again. She screamed,

"You abandoned me!"

She angrily threw the plaque across the yard. Then she stood and looked up at the sky.

"This is all your fault!"

Silence.

"God, why? Why him? Why not me?"

Silence.

"Why did you do this? What's good about this? If you're such a great and powerful God, then why did you do this?"

There was a slight breeze and Genie fell to her knees.

"Why?"

Carson had been acting a little strange. When he called, Genie would be short with him so that he'd hang up but the last time he called he sounded angry. When Genie picked up the phone she said,

"Hello?"

"Don't talk, just listen," Carson said.

She was surprised by his forcefulness.

"You and Tyler had something, it was obvious. When I met, you stopped talking to him. I thought it was because you liked me a lot and didn't have time for him."

That sounded right on the money, she thought.

He continued, "When he died, it was obvious that you loved him. I have no idea what made you come to me when you loved him. I'm still trying to figure out why you'd do that to me. Anyway, I was in love with you and it killed me to see you that hurt. I couldn't do anything to help either. You didn't want my help. But what hurt me the most is that you were that hurt because of another guy. So, think about that."

He hung up.

Genie walked into Blake's Brews and was enveloped into the calming scent of coffee and cocoa. She approached the counter.

"Hi, I wish to purchase a book."

The man working the counter smiled, "Which book would you like to buy?"

"I'll go get it," she said. She turned away from the counter. Hanging over the fireplace was a small picture of Tyler. There was a small note card under it,

"Always in our hearts."

Genie tried not to cry. Her throat went dry. She went to the back of the store and pulled a large book from the shelf. She brought it to the counter.

"This the one?"

The man asked her while pouring a cup of coffee.

"Yes. This is it," she said. He took the book and scanned it.

"That'll be twenty-one dollars and twenty-two cents."

Genie handed him the cash and took the book. As she was leaving, a firm hand grabbed her shoulder. She turned around and Arnold was standing behind her.

"Hello, Genesis."

"Hi, Mr. Arnold."

He looked sick. There were dark circles under his eyes and he'd lost too much weight. Had he always looked that sick? Arnold had dealt with loss before. He had loved Victor like a brother and he barely knew Tyler but he seemed just as affected and upset about Tyler's death.

"You haven't been back to write for us in a while."

She could feel the pain in his voice. Arnold was in pain, not physical pain, mental pain.

"Yeah, I'm really sorry. I was busy. School has been a little tough lately."

"Oh," he said rubbing the back of his neck, "Well, I have a favor to ask of you."

"Sure, anything you need."

He tensed up.

"I'd like you to write about Tyler."

Genie nodded.

"I'll bring it to the funeral tomorrow."

She turned to walk away but Arnold put out his hand and stopped her, "I'm sorry."

Genie turned to look at him, a tear gliding down her cheek.

"For what?" she questioned.

On her way home, she made a stop. She parked her car at the top of the hill that led down to the pier. There were flowers and crosses piled up at the top of the hill where Tyler's truck had gone over the guardrail. They had removed the truck from the water a few days after the crash. The guardrail stood, mangled and beaten. Genie stopped and stared.

This is where it ended. Where his life was basically over. He died in the hospital but his emotions, his thoughts, his movement, they ended here.

She walked down the hill to the pier. She followed it until the end and sat with her legs dangling over the side. This used to be her favorite place to come and sit. Now it seemed like an eerie reminder of Carson and Tyler, two memories that didn't mix. The waves tossed and turned. It used to seem like a calm part of nature but nothing in the water looked calm anymore. The same beauty that she had seen in the water before, made her think of the violent and tragic way that Tyler had died. He almost drowned in the water. He made it to the hospital but couldn't make it any farther. Well, he went somewhere after the hospital but Genie didn't know where. She guessed heaven. She sat and thought about all that had happened. She thought about what Addie and Carson had said to her. Did she love him before she met Carson? Was Carson the first guy she loved or was Tyler? Everyone being mad at her didn't bother her. Her emotions seemed numb lately, almost as if she didn't have any at all. She felt like a robot, something that didn't feel anything at all. She looked down into the water. Something gold caught her eye. The water was murky but shallow. She leaned over to see what it was.

About seven feet into the water, there was a trophy sitting on the bottom. There were other pieces of metal and tire shreds and things like that. The trophy had a mini racer at the top of it. It was the trophy that Noah had won. Tyler was bringing it home when he crashed. Noah had won first place. The trophy was another eerie reminder of what life was before he died. The water was murky but the metal stood out. The water was the tears that she cried and the very reason that she cried those tears.

She sat staring at a piece of notebook paper. What was the best way to write about Tyler? She tapped her pen on her desk. She thought of something and began to write. The words came easily after that and they all flowed onto the page. She reread what she had written and smiled. She looked in her closet and saw the black dress. She didn't want to wear it before, but now she had no choice. It was just part of life. She glanced back at the book she'd bought at Blake's and opened it up. She had an idea. She'd need a lot of manpower to make it happen. She grabbed her cell phone and flipped it open. She hit call. "Hello?" His voice sounded groggy, like she'd woken him up. What time was it anyway?

"Hi, Carson? I need your help."
    She explained her plan and he said he was on his way.
    She called the next person.
"Hellooo?"
    "Lindsey, it's Genie Anderson."
    "What do you want?"
    It was taking everything she had to not snap at Lindsey.
    "I need your help."
    They hung up and Genie walked into Noah's room. He was sitting on his bed, his head buried in a pillow.
    "Noah, you wanna help me with something?"
    Noah lifted his head in question.

Chapter 25

Genie walked into St. Bernadette's with her head held high. Everyone from school was sitting in the back. All family and close friends were sitting in the front, closest to the coffin. Mason, Michael, Alicia, Aidan, Bailey, Molly, Michelle, Carson's friends, the football team, the cheerleaders, and everyone else from Blakeridge was sitting in the last ten rows of pews. They had their school pins on each of their black suits and dresses.

Other people from town were seated in the middle rows. Arnold, Margaret, the owner of Blake's Brews, and the teachers from the schools were all seated and eyeing the funeral program.

They turned and stared as Genie approached Father Duggan.

"Hey, I need to hang something up, would you mind if we did?"

He lifted his head and looked at Genie.

"Sure," he said calmly.

He looked upset just as the whole town did. He glanced down at the coffin. It was closed.

"Thank you," she said.

She stepped away and walked to the entrance. She went out to where Carson had parked his car. Veronica, Lindsey, and Noah were standing with him by the car.

"He said it was okay, let's bring it in."

Each one of them grabbed a part of the large, rolled up cloth. They moved together and brought it down the main isle of the church. Each person in the church watched as the group moved forward. When they came to the coffin, Genie stopped and looked at the wooden surface.

"This one's for you."

They moved forward once again and hooked some wire to the top corners. The assembly watched as they pulled the wire back and lifted the cloth high above the crowd. Slowly, the cloth unraveled, revealing what they had created. Each person in the crowd eyed it and clapped.

Hanging above the coffin was an enormous cloth that had a toucan painted on it. It was beautifully painted with red, orange, and yellow accents. It was outlined in glitter. In the background was painted a pine box racer. Above the toucan and tropical flowers was written in fancy script, "And colorful as he was, he never let anyone see his true colors." Genie looked over the crowd who didn't see the significance in it but they didn't need to. She understood how important it was, and that was all that mattered. Lindsey smiled at her and mouthed, "Thank you."

Noah had a smile that stretch from ear to ear. Carson was proud of what he had painted. It was gorgeous. He had done an amazing job. He apologized for being so angry with her. He said that he understood that she couldn't help it. It felt good to know that at least he wasn't angry. Lindsey had added the glitter but that's all she could do. Veronica had her arm around Carson. She patted him on the back. She had never met Tyler but all parents have compassion for the death of a child. It was incredibly difficult to lose a child to death and to a terrible circumstance. Veronica looked over the artwork and she was clearly thinking of Landon. It must have been so difficult to lose her son to the man she had thought she loved. It's funny what love can cause. Veronica had one tear that was rolling down her cheek. She didn't look upset. She just looked content. Genie smiled. She eyed the book that Tyler had showed her. It was leaning against the coffin along with other memorabilia of Tyler's. She was thinking of what it must have looked like, her father giving Tyler the book. What Tyler had said rang in her head,

"He said that he saw a lot of potential and that he knew that I'd be around for a while."

How long was a while? Not quite long enough. She eyed the cloth banner. It had taken them until one this morning to finish it. Carson had brought the paints. Veronica had instructed them on how to make this work. Noah watched and did small things to help, like refilling the water dish or getting them lemonade or coffee. She watched her brother run to Ellen who was standing in the middle of the isle. He was finally smiling. Genie smiled and walked to her mother. She hugged them both. Arnold tapped Genie on the shoulder.

"Do you have the article?"

She nodded and replied, "Let me get it."

She ran to the book. She had slid the paper inside the book and forgotten to take it out. She pulled it out. Arnold took it and read it.

"This is wonderful. It will be in Sunday's paper."

She smiled.

"Oh, remember, the Maryland writing competition essays must be turned in tomorrow."

Genie's stomach flipped. She hadn't even started it.

"Oh, right. Thank you."

Ellen looked at her, one eyebrow raised.

"What competition?"

"I'll tell you later."

The organ began to play <u>Amazing Grace</u> and everyone sat. When Genie looked back to the entrance, Trinity was standing by the doors. Where had she come from? She was supposed to be leaving for Indonesia today. Trinity smiled and waved. Genie sat back in the pew and cried. Father Duggan stood sternly over the congregation. That same life that had danced in his eyes seemed to be lost now. Genie looked up at the cross. A statue of Jesus hung on the cross. She thought to herself, Jesus died just like Tyler did, painfully and too soon. It didn't seem quite right. The church that she came to every Sunday didn't seem the same as it had before. It was as if a dark cloud loomed over the building and prevented anyone under the cloud from ever being happy again. Everyone that surrounded her was in black. They all seemed awkward in their clothes and in their seat but comfortable in their tears. Father Duggan said the funeral and the burial was a little tough to take. The pallbearers were two of Tyler's uncles and four guys off of the football team. They each stood on a side of the coffin. They lifted it and brought it outside the doors of the church and slid it into the hearse. It didn't seem like Tyler was in there. It was just a wooden box.

The procession to the cemetery was eerily quiet. No one in town had missed the funeral, so the streets were bare. No one was sitting on their porch or gardening. When Ellen's car passed the high school, it seemed scary to see no activity inside the beautiful, brick building. It seemed as though every car in town was part of the line but slowly branched off onto neighborhood streets. Some people didn't want to see the burial. Noah didn't go to the burial because it would be too difficult for him to watch. Trinity drove him back to the house and stayed with him there. Genie stood and watched them bury Tyler. They lowered his coffin into the ground slowly. It was hard to imagine that just a week ago, he was alive and helping Noah put the finishing touches on his racer. That same body was being lowered into a dirt hole in the ground. It was almost unbelievable. She leaned over and looked at the wooden coffin sitting at the bottom of the six-foot grave. She stepped back and let them finish burying him. Addie was standing with her mother, bawling. Mr. Moore didn't do anything. He didn't cry, talk, or move. He was like a robot that had been brought out against his will. Mrs. Moore just took deep breaths and you could tell that she had no idea what to do. After the burial was over, Ellen started walking towards the car.

"Hey, mom, I'll be home in a little bit."

Ellen nodded and continued walking toward the parking lot. Genie took a look at the grave marker.

"Tyler Joseph Moore. January 4, 1990-April 9, 2006."

She looked at the fresh dirt.

"Goodbye, Camo."

The glittered ribbon in her hair swayed in the wind. It danced in the wind and its movements were just as hopeless and uncontrollable as life was. It was hard to believe that someone that lived for only sixteen years was already gone. He hadn't chosen death. It chose him. The church had always said that God had a will for us. What was Tyler's? What had he done to deserve this? Why did he only live for sixteen years? There were terrible people out there who live to be eighty, or more. It wasn't fair. He'd been a great person; an inspiring person. Why did he have to die when others got to live? She turned away from his grave and walked a good 50 feet before she came to her father's grave. The blue hydrangeas she had brought a little over a week ago were still there. They were wilted a little bit but they were still alive. She sat down and leaned against the tree.

"Hey, dad."

Silence.

"I'm sorry I said you abandoned me earlier. I was upset. I'm still trying to figure this whole death thing out."

Silence.

"I realized that you didn't abandon me at all . . . you've been here all long."

Chapter 26

Genie sat and stared at her laptop. This time, she didn't have writer's block. She typed away. She thought about Carson and how much she loved him. She thought about Tyler and whether or not she loved him. She questioned whether Carson was her first love or not. Should she have been with Tyler? It was hard to believe that she would never have a chance to find that out. She came up with her question. She wrote for hours. She knew that she did her best. It didn't matter if she won the Junior Writing Competition. The question she thought of made her think about her whole life and everyone in it. She didn't care about the competition and winning. She walked to the mailbox and looked up at the sky and wondered if her father, Tyler, and God were watching. She figured that they must be, because it didn't seem possible for her to live without someone watching her. She slid the envelope in the mailbox and stepped away from it. She knew she wasn't going to win, but it didn't matter. She had accomplished a lot by simply writing the essay in the first place. She realized she wasn't alone.

Genie was walking home from the coffee shop when she saw Addie. Addie was walking alone and Genie stopped her.

"Hey."

Addie whipped around and glared at her. Her face had been paler than usual. Her beautiful hair looked greasy, like it hadn't been washed in days. Her once glowing eyes seemed lifeless and sad.

"Don't talk to me," she scolded.

Genie was stunned.

"What's wrong?"

Addie looked crazy.

"What's wrong? What's wrong! My brother is dead!"

"I know that! You don't think I miss him!"

Genie looked equally as crazed. Addie's eyes filled with rage.

"You didn't seem to miss him before he died!"

It felt like Genie had been stabbed in the heart. She could barely breathe.

"What do you mean?"

"You left him to go hang out with Carson. You don't think that hurt him?!" Addie questioned.

"I'm sorry! You don't think I regret everything I said to him?"

"You didn't have to see him cry over you! Seeing him hurt makes it really easy to hate you," she screamed.

Addie pointed at her and made large gestures. Genie was silent. She wanted to say something but she didn't know how. Her throat closed up.

Addie screamed through her tears.

"He loved you! And you let him down!"

She stormed off.

Genie could feel a large lump in her throat. She couldn't speak and Addie was already long gone. He loved her. She had gone off to be with Carson and he loved her. How could she not see that? There was nothing she could do now.

Ellen sat in her bedroom and cried every night after dinner. She would scream and curse God for taking away so many people from her. She said that it wasn't fair. She had done the same thing when Victor died. She was a mess. She was questioning her faith. How could a woman who survived her husband's death with faith and strength be giving in now? She named her children religious names, Trinity, The Father, Son, and Holy Spirit, Genesis the first book in the Bible. Then there was Noah, being the story of Noah and the Ark. Ellen thrived in her faith. What made her quit now? She asked God if he had a plan for her. She asked Him why he had taken such a young child in such a brutal way. She just kept asking Him why. Noah was doing a little better. He had gone back to school. He had gotten back to normal a little.

Trinity had been staying in Genie's room. They were best friends. When Trinity showed up at the funeral then explained why she didn't go on the trip, it made Genie realize that she was a normal human being. She breathed the same air and she suffered the same pain. That night after the funeral, Genie and Trinity stayed up and talked about their father. Trinity explained that when Victor died, she comforted Ellen and did her best to care for her. There's no right way to care for someone who is grieving. When Trinity said this, Genie understood that it meant that there was no wrong way either. It was a part of life. There are no answers. Trinity also explained that she didn't suck up to mom because she wanted to be the perfect daughter and try to make everyone look bad, she just did it because she had no choice. If she misbehaved, Ellen wouldn't have been able to handle it. She acted perfect because someone had to make it a little easier on Mom. She and

Trinity had begun to grow close and they had more in common than Genie had originally thought. They watched movies together and did each other's hair. They talked about college and what was going on in school. Genie had returned to school.

She talked to Addie a little more each day. They would never be friends like they had been but they would always share the common bond of Tyler just as they had met that way.

Carson and Genie had faded away from each other. It hurt a little but there was something about Carson that she felt was wrong. Every time she saw him, she saw the scar and it was only a reminder of what Tyler had done for her. It felt like if she went back to Carson, she was betraying Tyler. She saw him in the hallway. He always looked a little distraught but little by little things went back to normal.

One day, she was typing up a research paper and she went on Google. Instead of typing in 'The Great Depression' she typed in 'Tyler Moore.' There were over 1,000 results. Each link said something about R.I.P or what he had done for his school and church community. Someone had even started a website about him. He touched so many people's lives and it was evident that Genie wasn't the only one who thought about him.

Tyler's locker had been cleaned out and his books had been turned back into the school. No one sat in the desk that he sat in for his classes. It was as if he was never there. Carson had made a painting in memory of Tyler and it was hanging when you first walked in the school. It was a watercolor painting of Tyler. In the background were what seemed to be lights. It was beautiful and she couldn't have imagined a better depiction of Tyler's essence. Carson had done a great job and he was going to go far as an artist. She did miss Carson a lot but she didn't want to go up to him. It just didn't seem right. It wouldn't be the same. Things just weren't ever going to be the same.

For a long time after the funeral, Genie didn't go to church. She didn't know if she believed in God. If there was a God, why did He do this? Why would He hurt so many people? Why were there natural disasters? Why was there crime? It didn't make sense.

One day, when Genie was walking back after turning in one of her pieces to Arnold, she saw Father Duggan mailing something. He stopped and looked at her.

"Genesis. I haven't seen you in a long time. How have you been?"

"I've been better. I'm just trying to get by."

"Well, there's no fun in living just to survive and get by," he said.

"Life isn't too fun at all right now."

He looked down at his shoes then back at her.

"Come with me, I think we should talk."

Genie followed him back to the church a few blocks away. It was late April and the weather had cleared up. The sun was shining and the air was warm. Father Duggan set his bag of groceries down on the steps of St. Bernadette's and gestured for Genie to sit.

"I know how hard this is."

"I just don't understand why God did this," she said.

"I didn't either. When I lost my parents, I questioned my faith as well. I think God kind of expects us to doubt him."

"Why?"

"Genesis, I've learned that you can't tell how strong someone is until they're faced with a challenge. God puts bad things in the world so that we can determine the good people from the bad. If there were no crime and no problems, we'd never have heroes. If there were no issues in the world, we would never know how far we, as humans, would go to help our fellow man. Now, I know this sounds crazy but something good has come out of Tyler's death. Do you remember the candle light service?"

"Yeah."

"If Tyler didn't die, we would never have gotten to see our entire town come together like that. Death unites people. As sad as it is, death helps to bond every human on earth together. Everyone dies which means that every single person on this earth will lose someone they love or care for. It's sad but there's something comforting in knowing you are not alone. That candle light service was an example of everyone showing you and the Moore's and everyone that knew Tyler, you are not alone."

"Why Tyler though?"

"You see, everyone has a purpose. God puts us here with a very specific purpose. Some complete their mission and some don't ever understand it. There is a reason you are here, Genie. Well, God has us come home once we have done our job. It's our goal to go back to him once we've done our job. But, only he decides when that is. Tyler must have completed his mission. Did you learn anything from Tyler?"

"Yeah, a lot actually."

"And when you looked around at his funeral, were there other people there?"

"Yeah, you were there. You saw how many people were there. There were a lot."

"Everyone who showed up that day and even some who didn't were touched by Tyler. He made an impact on every single person there's life. Now tell me, why Tyler?"

"It was his time."

"That's right Genesis. There's a reason for everything. You have to trust God. You must have faith."

Right then and there, Genie's faith was back.

Chapter 27

The Anderson family sat and ate dinner.

"Pass the salt."

Noah's little arm reached over the table and pushed the salt to Genie.

Ellen had gone back to work and was happier than she had been in a long time. She must have found closure. Trinity had gone back to college but she wasn't going to Indonesia. She had given up the opportunity to come and comfort Genie after Tyler died. She was the best sister anyone could ask for. It ended up being that she wasn't a terrible sister; she was just trying too hard which made her come off as a little annoying.

Ellen hadn't been too pleased about Trinity not going on the trip so it kind of made Trinity's not being perfect, official.

Poppy was doing as he always did. He was fine.

Noah was great, just a great kid and right on cue said, "Dinner's great, Mom, thanks." Ellen smiled.

Out of the blue, the doorbell rang. Ellen looked around the table, questioningly. Genie got up and answered the door. The mailman was holding a manila envelope. He had dark bags under his eyes and it was clear that this was his last stop.

"Sorry, this one came a little late and it said urgent on it."

"Oh," Genie said taking the envelope, "Thanks."

She shut the door and walked through the living room, staring at it. She opened it and grasped a cream letter that had come with it. Her eyes scanned the letter.

"Oh my gosh," she said.

"What? What is it?" Ellen said rising from her chair.

"I won." Genie smiled.

"Won what?" questioned Ellen Genie smiled.

"The Maryland Writing Competition. I won."

Ellen hugged her and whispered in her ear, "I'm so proud of you, Genie."

She had never said that before. Genie smiled.

"There's a phone number, they want me to call them about something."

She walked over to the phone and dialed the number on the paper.

"Hello, yes, this is Genesis Anderson . . . Yes, I won the Junior Writing competition . . . The letter said to call . . . When? . . . Okay . . . That sounds great . . . What time? . . . I'll be there. Thank you very much . . . Bye."

Noah, Ellen, and Poppy watched in anticipation as she hung up the phone.

"They want me to come and present my essay in front of a psychology class."

"Oh my Lord!" Ellen grabbed her and hugged her again.

"What was your essay even on?"

Chapter 28

Genie stood in front of one hundred and fifty students. She took deep breaths, trying to imagine everyone in their underwear.

The man at the podium was introducing her, "Students, this is Genesis Anderson. She won the Junior Writing Competition for her wonderful essay. She is going to talk about her essay with you today. Give her your full attention."

He walked over to where Genie was standing and nudged her, "you're on."

She walked up to the podium and a copy of her essay was there waiting for her. She looked out over the crowd. She tried to think about her mom, Noah, Trinity, and Addie. She took one last deep breath and eyed her audience. There were a lot of new faces but there was one familiar one. Carson stood leaning against the back wall. She hadn't asked him to come but she was glad he was there.

She began, "Hi, I'm Genie. I have one simple question, 'What is love?' This is a commonly asked question but there is no real answer. We all can share what we think and what our opinion is but there is no definite answer. There have been thousands of movies made about it and countless songs. It's something that everyone thinks about or comes across everyday. Do we even know what it is? Webster's dictionary defines love as an intense feeling of deep affection. That doesn't seem quite right. Love is so much more that. Love is more than a word. Love is the bond between people all over the world. It is what unites us. Love is the bond we have with each person we meet. We have to love everyone. Love is not something you experience once in your life. You experience it millions of times. But not all love is the same. The stranger walking down the street, you love them for a different reason than you love your husband or wife. There is a difference between being in love and loving. Loving someone is caring for them and wanting them to be safe and happy. I love my mother, my sister, my grandfather, my brother, my teachers, my friends, and I could go on forever. Most people have only been in love once. This is the love you have for your spouse or your boyfriend or girlfriend or your fiancé. Sometimes it's not about being in love with one person. It's about sharing love with every person you meet. I just learned this lesson recently and not many people understand it. I have only met one other person who understands this.

A good friend of mine, Tyler, loved everyone and treated everyone with a certain respect. He understood what it meant to love every person you meet. Unfortunately, he was unable to share this wisdom with me because he was killed tragically in a car accident. His sister came to me after he had passed and said, 'He loved you.' I did not understand what she meant until now. He wasn't in love with me. He loved me like he loved everyone. Being a child of God is loving everyone and treating him or her with respect. That's what love is. It's not sex. It's not roses and candies on Valentine's Day, and it's not just marriage. It's an everyday aspect of life. Saying I love you doesn't mean you're in love with a person. You can say I love you to anyone. When you cannot imagine your life without a person, that's when you are in love with them. So my question, "What is love," is not answerable. It's just one simple question."

Edwards Brothers,Inc!
Thorofare, NJ 08086
22 March, 2011
BA2011081